THE LIGHT FROM THE STONE

Richard Kipling

Published by

Llyfrau Cambria Books, Wales, United Kingdom.

Cambria Books is a division of

Cambria Publishing.

Discover our other books at: www.cambriabooks.co.uk

Dedication

To the Rhosygilwen writing group and all the friends who helped along the way.

CONTENTS

Chapter 1

Daniel sensed where the fish was, though the water was like a mirror. It reflected the trees, his bronzed face, his grey eyes, his hand clutching a sharpened stick. There. With a deft movement he drove the weapon down, piercing the river's skin, plunging deep. When he drew it back there was a trout impaled on it, its scales glistening in the sun. Another kill. That was the way of it now. Fish, rabbits. An old man. Pulling the fish from the stick, he put his thumb into its mouth to gain purchase and snapped its neck.

A small canvas sheet and a knife lay at his side with two more fish, still twitching. Three was enough, and he wrapped them in the canvas. Then he cast the white petals of wood he had pared from the hunting stake into the water, wiped the knife on the grass and slid it into a leather sheath at his waist. Eager to leave, he hardly looked down as he packed. He knew he was vulnerable during a hunt, concentrating on his quarry: its behaviour, its movements, its perception of the world. Now his eyes scanned the far bank of the river, the crowded trees behind. He stood, stowed the fish in his knapsack and slung it on his back over a camouflage jacket. Then he jogged back into the woods. His feet were bare, hardened against the sharpest thorns, and he moved on them lightly. The power in his frame made him seem taller than the six feet he was, and yet, weaving between the trees he became little more than a shadow.

"What about posh-boy?"

"That Daniel?"

"Yeah, him. You got a light?"

There was the squeak of a window being opened.

"Didn't say, much did he?"

"Not much of interest."

The smell of cigarette smoke drifted in through Daniel's bedroom window. The rest of campus was quiet, just this one conversation audible through the wall separating his room from the kitchen.

"'I didn't go to school, my father educated me.'"

Smirking laughter broke the stillness of the night.

"Give him a chance Jamie, he seemed nice."

A girl's voice – Jane? He thought that was her name, but he'd only spoken to them all briefly. He was the latecomer, turning up at the end of Fresher's week when they'd all been there from the start.

"Nice eh?" More stifled laughter.

"Shut up. The walls aren't that thick. What if he hears you?"

"He's asleep, cuddled up with his teddy I bet."

"Jamie! Drop it. What did you think of the bar anyway?"

"Did you see that cross he was wearing?"

"Just leave it."

That cross – his mum had given it to him as a leaving present. Passed down from his grandma. The conversation droned on, petered out, ended with the scraping of chairs and the banging of doors. Steps reverberating down the metal stairs – Jane on the way back to her block. A toilet flushing somewhere. Then back to silence, darkness.

The next day he went to the college welcome event on his own. The common room was carefully blank: cream walls and an un-patterned blue carpet like an empty sea. Upon this ocean were cast rafts of Freshers beginning, awkwardly, to introduce themselves to each other. The buffet – free, like the bait in a trap – was laid out along one long wall, offering meat paste sandwiches and mean little Vol-au-vents, aptly dried out by the air-conditioning. Daniel hovered by the table, looking around him uncertainly. He was thin and pale, with carefully combed brown hair that he kept brushing back from his ears with his hands. The plates were emptying, and he was running out of excuses for not moving. He eyed the nearest group to him; the circle they formed was not quite closed. He could just walk over –

"Hello old chap."

A tall man with receding hair and a pale face looked down at him. Daniel had a blank moment, adjusting his focus.

"I'm Bill, the Dean." The man held out a long, thin hand.

"Daniel."

"Good to meet you, Daniel. Your cross caught my eye – nice to see."

He'd made sure he pinned it on again. He hadn't intended to until last night – he'd wanted to keep it for church, for special occasions.

"Tell me, what are you here to study?"

"Biological science. I just want to get started on the work really."

"Enthusiasm! I like your attitude. Where did you go to school?"

Daniel blushed. "Actually, my parents taught me."

"Well, your attitude is a credit to them old chap. And this is a good place for Biology."

"Yes, my dad said the same – it was one of the reasons I came."

"Thanks." The Dean took a pastry from an attendant who was offering them around. "Can I ask why you wanted to read biology?"

"I want to get into crop breeding, eventually I mean."

"Sowing and reaping, lots of Biblical metaphor there." The Dean glanced at his cross again. "Which church do you go to, if you don't mind me asking?"

"Well, I only arrived yesterday –"

"Of course, of course, stupid of me."

"I checked online though: I think it's St James' I'll be attending."

"I knew it! My wife and I go there. God has a way of bringing the right people together, don't you think? Well, tell you what, if you come to the 10.30am mass you can join me and Susanne – that's my wife – for a cup of tea afterwards."

"Oh," Daniel blushed again. "Thanks."

"Great!" Bill glanced across the room. "Daniel, I have to go, people I need to talk to. But I'll see you at the weekend." He held out his hand. "Good to meet you." And he was gone, stalking away to engage someone else in conversation. Across the carpet laughter rose from the little group of students Daniel had almost joined.

Stepping out of the building a few minutes later Daniel fumbled with the zip of his waxed jacket, doing it up to the top against the cold wind that drove over the green, round the concrete angles of the students' union, leaves flying with it like dried-out birds. He followed them, joining a steady trickle of others going to register and collect their student cards. He was conscious of the sophisticated long trench coats and fashionably shabby jeans worn by his fellows, the elegant roll neck sweaters and high boots of the girls. Conscious of himself scuttling along in his rural gear, like a gamekeeper out to check the pheasant pens. He kept his head down. Once inside he took his coat off and tried to blend in, shuffling into the first queue (registration forms). There was a smell of floor polish and a melee of voices; the bored tones of the administrators, the laughter of new groups of friends vying with each other for attention.

The foyer was like an underground carpark, with grey ramps leading to other floors, strip lights above, vending machines like sentinels lining the side walls, green plastic seats in rows bolted to the floor facing them. At the centre was a line of desks, each one for a different range of names. The queue divided and he joined the one

4

heading towards 'his' desk. 'O' for Orpheus. He tapped his heel nervously. There were a lot of people. He looked back towards the doors.

"Hi." The girl behind him in the queue smiled. It was Jane.

"Hi." He couldn't think of anything else to say, and just looked at her for a moment. She had green eyes.

"I think the queue's moved."

"Oh." He turned and made up the ground.

"So, what course are you here for?" Her voice dragged him back around to face her, thrilled and fearful.

"Biology."

"Me too! I'm sorry, we didn't have chance to say hello properly last night." She held out her hand; it was still cold from her being outside.

Say something else. Think of something.

"NEXT," the administrator called out, and he was forced to turn away again. Jane moved up next to him, and he fumbled to find his ID. She had finished filling in her form before he had completed half of his, and had disappeared into the crowd by the time he turned away with his new student card in his hand.

∗

The first few days of term passed quickly – the introductory lectures and events, the awkward social ice-breakers. Daniel struggled to connect with the students on his corridor, unwilling to go out drinking and, as a result, left outside the group. Now it was Sunday morning and Bill, Susanne and he were walking back along the tree-lined avenue between the church and the Peters' house, crunching through brown and gold leaves and scattered conker casings that lay on the concrete like tiny green mines.

5

"I think you'll really get on with the church student society Daniel." The Dean walked with long, loping strides.

"Yes, they seemed like nice people."

They'd added him to their social media group to help with a a sponsored walk for communities in central Africa facing an ebola outbreak. He finally felt he had some chance to be part of something.

"And what did you think of Father Davies?" asked Susanne. "I always think he gets over his thoughts so well ..."

"Yes, he seemed nice – his sermon was very clear."

He'd almost fallen asleep during it – halls had been noisy last night.

"Here we are!" Bill moved ahead as they turned into the drive to unlock the front door of the house

Susanne ushered Daniel in. "Welcome."

A wave of warm air, heavy with the smell of fresh cakes and flowers washed over him. Over tea in the front room, Susanne asked him about his first week.

"You must have been nervous."

"It's very different from home."

"Of course it is – so many people and things to learn. I expect you feel better now you've been to church and got to know a few people there – a bit more at home."

"And how were your first lectures Daniel?" Bill asked as he cut into a slice of sponge cake with one of the ornate little forks Susanne had laid out for them.

Daniel paused; it wasn't an easy question to answer. Some of it he'd enjoyed. He understood most of the detail: his parents had been good teachers. But the ideas that went with it hadn't always been familiar. "Mostly they've been good. No assignments yet, but

6

I've got my reading lists."

"Who's teaching the course this year?"

Daniel thought for a second. "I think Dr Weldon, Professor Teal and Professor Pembrey, but it's hard to remember all the names."

"There's a trick to it old chap. When someone introduces themselves, notice something particular about them – like do they have a moustache or do they wear glasses – and think of something their name rhymes with. Works for me."

"Who's Pembrey?" asked Susanne.

"Do you mean Pemberton by any chance?"

"Yes, Pemberton, sorry." It was Pemberton whose ideas had surprised him.

"What did you make of him?" Asked Bill, fixing him with his pale eyes. It felt like a test.

"Honestly, some of what he teaches doesn't fit with what my parents taught me." Daniel shifted uneasily at the admission. Maybe he was too far behind to step up. Struggling after a week, even before he thought about the social side. But the Dean didn't look disappointed.

"I would have been surprised if they had Daniel. Your parents kept everything in its place I suppose. Kept science out of religion. Quite right. But it's not enough for some people now."

"Remember your parents' lessons Daniel," Susanne interjected. "Don't let Pemberton knock your beliefs."

"He's made you doubt yourself old chap, I can see that." Bill leant back in his chair, his cake finished. "Well, Susanne and I are here to support you. And so is God. Keep your faith."

*

In the forest he found an outcrop of rock and gazed along its steep face. It was too high for anyone to jump down from, a safe place to stop and eat if he sat in close, protected on one side. He strode along its foot to a place where an ash tree erupted from a fissure above his head, its yellow-green leaves shading the grass and moss below. The vegetation was flattened; this was probably a resting place for a deer or a badger. He sat down, propping himself against the cold rock, feeling its solidity.

The urge to move rose up in him almost as soon as he settled. Like an itch. He was never free of it these days. He ignored it, took out his knife, un-wrapped the fish and began to gut them with instinctive precision. When he was done, he took the entrails and flung them into the woods — scattering them, so they would look like something left by an animal. He collected firewood, hooking it up with long, strong fingers. Picking up a flat rock, he carried it to where the ash spread its hands of living wood and placed it down to one side of the tree, so the flames from the fire wouldn't catch those arboreal limbs.

With moss and bark as tinder he began the lighting ritual, sowing the seed of the fire with flint and metal, cupping the dry material in his hands, cradling the smouldering, flickering ember-light until it caught. Soon the wood crackled amid flames that called out to be fed, but he gave them only scraps of fuel. The bigger the fire the more smoke and light there would be and the greater danger of it being noticed. He skewered the fish lengthwise on stripped alder sticks. By burying one end of each stick into the soil he could let the fish stand and cook slowly over the flame. He sat silently, watching the silver scales tarnish and brown.

*

"What Darwin, what Watson and Crick and all those pioneers of the modern evolutionary synthesis showed, was that we are made of the same stuff as all other organisms, that we are related to all of them, evolved from a common ancestor that was no more than self-replicating slime in a pond."

Week five, and Pemberton in full flow again. Daniel wrote it all down, of course. He needed to pass the module.

"We are shaped by our genes, and they evolve through selection; competition from other individuals and other species, the requirements of our environment all acting to remove the weakest genotypes. Our physical form and our behaviour evolved in this way, over the generations. Therefore, both our physical attributes and behaviour can be explained using the logic of selection and the methods of the modern life sciences."

No room for freedom? What would be the point of it all?

Around him, the silence that the lecture had spun over the auditorium disintegrated as Pemberton concluded. He was good, Daniel had to admit that. He packed his notes into his backpack, already loaded with books, and edged out of the row – he always sat near the front, so there was nobody to wait for. The others were tumbling down the steps in a cascade of noise and colour, and he fled before them, out of the heavy double doors and into the corridor. Someone pushed their way out behind him –

"Daniel!"

He recognised the voice and was immediately anxious.

"Jane! Hi."

"I wondered," she paused with a smile as they stood aside to let the other students flow past them. Daniel had a desire to dive into that stream and be lost. "– I wondered if you'd like to go over these notes with me later. Pemberton confuses me a bit. It might help to talk through it."

Just what he had been wanting, someone to talk it over with – and Jane, with her long dark hair and pretty eyes. But the rising warmth was pushed back by a knot of fear. This was the third time she'd asked him to meet up with her, and each time that fear welled up. Usually he could avoid it – she went out with Dave and the others, but after that first night he had kept out of their way and silenced the constant messages from their group chat. And her room was in another block. Why was it all so difficult? Back home there had been no girls, no real friends – just woods and fields, the grounds of his parents' house, church.

"Thanks, but I've got something on tonight. We should though, sometime…" He trailed off, looked down the corridor. "Anyway, I've got to run – I've got another lecture."

He hadn't. He walked away quickly before she could look at him and see he was lying. *Why are you walking away?* He pushed the thought down, turned his mind to his new assignment.

✳

Time passed – a month and a half of learning, of church and fundraising, of being kept awake by everyone coming back late from the clubs, of running from Jane and wanting to see her. Another Sunday. The tinkle of Susanne's teaspoon against her cup was as gentle as the soporific ticking of the clock on the mantelpiece. Daniel knew the place well now – beige walls, tastefully expensive furniture, gentle, carefully-chosen paintings, the porcelain animals, the reassuring embrace of a Georgian Townhouse, and Bill and Susanne, talking to him as a friend and not as a student, as if he had already made that jump into the security of academia.

"So, how's your week been Daniel?"

Bill's tall frame was folded beneath him in a zigzag as he lent forward in his armchair to reach for his cup and saucer.

"I'm good thanks – you know, just the usual lectures." He paused. He wanted to mention Jane but bottled out. "I had to listen to Pemberton again – 'humans are only animals.'"

"Do you have to take his lectures?" asked Susanne.

"Yes, they're core. But it's not a problem – it's just when he gets going, he's hard to argue against. And he *is* a good lecturer; he makes things interesting."

"Wide is the road, Daniel." She was serious.

"Well," Bill looked round at the bookshelf behind him, where works with titles like 'The light and the way' and 'A pilgrim's journey' were nestled alongside an array of light fiction and books on antiques and classic cars and flower arranging. "You might have to listen to it, but it doesn't mean you should be unprepared to defend your faith." He got up and picked out a couple of volumes and put them on the coffee table. "Take these and have a read. I didn't want to give them to you before, just as you were starting. But I think you can handle it now. Pemberton antidotes."

"It would be good – but the halls are so noisy I can't really concentrate on anything."

Or you can't think because of Jane.

Susanne frowned. "I think the porters should keep an eye on that sort of thing. Can't you do something Bill?"

"I can have a word with the Head Porter I suppose – if that would help old chap?"

"Well, if it's no trouble –" Daniel picked up his freshly poured tea and took a sip, reluctantly dispelling the taste of the Host and communion wine. Their little cup of tea after Mass had almost become a tradition already, somewhere to unburden his problems. Apart from in the darkness of the confessional, it was the only place he could.

"None at all."

"Thanks." He shifted against the cushions propped around him.

"But," Bill smiled at his wife. "I think our Daniel has something else on his mind."

He had. But he was reluctant to sour this world – the world of his faith, of tea, of Bill and Susanne, of his parents – the world of safety – with the taint of his new problems. The problem of Jane, the problem of his fellow students who laughed at his beliefs and his seriousness and his accent, who distrusted him for not getting drunk with them. But he couldn't avoid it now; Bill had scented his uneasiness.

"Come on Daniel, you've been quiet ever since you arrived. What is it?"

"Well, there *was* something else – I was going to ask Father Davies, but ..." He struggled for the right phrase. Bill saw his hesitation.

"Don't worry – Susanne and I know a bit about the world."

"OK," Daniel overcame his embarrassment. "It's this girl – " Bill smiled, Susanne frowned slightly.

"Her name's Jane."

"Go on," prompted Bill.

"It's – that is – I know she likes me, but I'm not sure what to do."

Susanne lent forward. "What sort of girl is she Daniel?"

"Well, she's nice, but ..."

"Does she go to church?"

"No, I don't think she's religious."

"Hmm. How well do you know her?"

"She's on a different course, but we have some modules together. She's asked me back to her room a few times, after lectures." Susanne's expression altered a little. "To help her with work I mean."

"And did you go?"

"No. I was embarrassed."

12

"Well, I think you were probably right not to. You can get hurt, getting involved too easily. You'll know when you find the right person."

"You think so?"

She put her hand on his knee. "Listen Daniel, you're special – look at the grades you came here with. You're clever enough to do really well. Focus on that and God will look after everything else. He knows the difference between what we might want and what we need. Just because you want something it doesn't mean it's right for you to have it."

"Yes, I suppose you're right."

Why can't you think for yourself for once?

"Susanne's got a good feel for these things old chap – work hard and things will come right. We have to rely on God's grace."

How would they know what God wants?

"Of course. I need to focus."

Bill smiled – "Anyway Daniel, to brighter things – have you been practicing your piano?"

"Yes, it's been good – I went down to the music school the other night."

"Great," Bill glanced at his wife. "Do you want to play us something now? You know how much Susanne likes it."

Before, Daniel had only played the piano with his dad but, once Susanne found out, she insisted he performed for them too. Her favourite was Rossini – Daniel had been working on 'The Thieving Magpie' for her. Bill led the way to the drawing room.

"Daniel, what will it be this week?" Susanne asked.

They crossed the hall and to a larger room, and there was the piano. He always got a thrill when he saw it; a Bechstein Grand, in

13

walnut, majestic on the polished floorboards. Today the sunlight streamed onto it through the bay windows, sliding off its smooth curves. It was a treat to sit himself on the stool, to put out his hands and touch the keys, imagining a little crowd filled the high-ceilinged, ornate room, not just Bill and Susanne sitting on the edge of an antique sofa. There was always a bunch of flowers on the mahogany side table, a gaudy selection of colours, frothing up and out of the cut-glass vase to scent the room, and the music and the fragrance would drift together in the stillness. He could forget everything else when he sat there. In his mind he was, as he had always been as a child, alongside his father. He felt the keys, cool beneath his fingers, the room silent around him, waiting to be filled. And he began to play, the jolly tune rippling out into the quiet, Susanne laughing delightedly at the first notes.

The sun beamed in, a winter sun but warm through the glass, and he had a feeling almost of floating. But after a minute or so a cloud cut that stream of light. The room darkened. From nowhere, a dull fear arose inside him. Suddenly he wanted to be at home. He wanted to be with his parents, not with Bill and Susanne. The joy of the moment disintegrated. He finished the piece, but it had lost all its gaiety.

"Daniel, is there something wrong?" Susanne had evidently noticed his expression.

"I don't know. I just suddenly felt – I don't know." The scent of flowers, moments ago uplifting, was cloying. "I'm sorry – I really have to go." He stood up.

"Are you sure you're alright old chap?"

"I'm fine, I just need a bit of fresh air, I think. Don't worry," he added, seeing the concern on their faces. "It's not to do with you. I just felt like – I don't know."

He made for the refuge of the college library. For the rest of the afternoon, he sat in the silent space of papery whispers, reading, taking in knowledge. For a while he forgot about the incident at the piano. Here was Mayr (one of the 'fathers of the Modern Evolutionary Synthesis' according to Pemberton) telling him how he believed genes were linked together, their uses intertwined – big changes requiring a genetic 'revolution'. From nowhere he remembered something a nun had once said to him, at the church back home 'God is the glue that binds everything together'. God in everything, everything interlinked. Mayr was safe, gentle almost, smoothing out the problems. Then he thought of old Pemberton again, staring out from the podium –

"Today, more and more scientists are freed enough from superstition and religion to see how things work, without the prejudices of culture getting in their way."

Like Dawkins cutting through the weak-minded under-brush of spirituality: the survival of genes explained everything, human beings just vehicles for their continuation. Harder than Mayr or his contemporary Haldane. Extremists. They crashed once more against the rock of his belief. But there was something in Mayr's ideas that was more pervasive. He pushed that thought back and reached into his bag for an old paperback he was halfway through.

Yes, hide from it. I expect that'll solve things.

He needed to read those books Bill had given him too. But not now, he couldn't face it somehow.

When he emerged it was dark. A deluge of autumn rain was falling in a rush onto the smooth paving stones of the quad. He pulled up the hood of his raincoat and hurried across the open space, wet leaves from the oak tree at its centre slippery underfoot, the sound of the downpour like the hiss of static all around him, blurring his senses. A couple of students ran under the archway ahead, laughing and soaked. Sheltered by the parapet of crumbling stone they stopped and kissed with the water a curtain in front of them. Daniel hurried past them, head down.

Just because you want something…

It was only about half an hour's walk to his halls, but before half that time had passed the temperature was beginning to fall, the rain turning to sleet, its slush on the pavements soaking through his shoes, the black skeletons of trees locked down and cold at the roadside. By the time he got in the noise from the shared kitchen told him the night was well underway: bangs and crashes, laughter. He went straight to his room and tried to think about his work. He was hungry but he wasn't about to get involved with the party. He would have to wait until they went out – shouldn't be long now. Then he realised he'd forgotten to buy bread. He'd have to go back out. He put his raincoat back on and left the sanctuary of his room. On the way back with a sliced wholemeal loaf under his arm, he ran into the others, seeing them too late to avoid it.

"Danny, you miserable sod, what're you up to?"

That was Devon (ridiculous name) in the equally ridiculous fancy dress he was incapable of doing without (tonight he seemed to be dressed as a northern factory worker from the nineteenth century). He was dragging Jamie who was imitating a dog, wearing a thin fake fur overall, oblivious to the freezing temperature – the skies had cleared above, clouds folding back and away to nothing.

"I was just getting some bread." He could almost feel their unspoken judgement of his voice, could imagine them mocking him in some dark, noisy pub, their tongues loosened by drink. Darkness, gnashing of teeth...

And you with a halo?

With them was Sarah, in her short Friday night skirt and, as if to round off his discomfort – Jane.

"Come to the pub Danny," shouted Devon.

"Let him go, you know he won't." The boys wandered off, Sarah in their wake. Jane hung back. There was a pause, but she'd obviously had enough drink not to feel awkward –

"Don't listen to them Daniel – why don't you come out?"

16

"No, I've got an essay to get started."

"We don't have to go with them – we could have a drink somewhere else, just me and you."

"No, no, I really have to do this work."

You soft git.

He saw her expression change imperceptibly, a shadow of disappointment that was quickly subsumed within the alcohol-glaze of her eyes. "Why don't you just come and have a bit of fun?"

"You go, I'm fine here. I need to get this done by tomorrow. There'll be other nights."

"But they won't be tonight."

He ignored that – "I'll see you tomorrow."

He watched her leaving as if from a distance. Back in the warmth of the empty halls it was good to be alone, to be able to sit in his dressing gown drinking proper filtered coffee, to read his textbooks with classical music playing. That was the way he liked his evenings; not like the nights of the formal college meals when he had to have dinner with them all and they dressed in the gowns they'd hadn't earned, and he was forced to listen to their nonsense. He took down his copy of the bible, its pages dog-eared from use.

"In the beginning God created the heaven and the earth. And the earth was without form, and void; and darkness was upon the face of the deep. And the Spirit of God moved upon the face of the waters."

How many times had his mum read those words to him, while they sat on the rug in front of the fire and he drank his night-time hot chocolate?

"And God made the beast of the earth after his kind, and cattle after their kind, and every thing that creepeth upon the earth after his kind: and God saw that it was good. And God said, Let us make man in our image, after our likeness: and let them have dominion over the fish of the sea, and over the fowl of the air, and over the cattle, and over all the earth, and over every creeping thing that creepeth upon the earth. So God created man in his own image, in the image of God created he him; male and female created he them."

There was no vagueness, no room for uncertainty. Mayr and the others were wrong. But still. There was a richness to their writing, a depth. Like the difference between a picture book and a novel. He broke away from that train of thought, went to the sink in the corner of the room and cleaned his teeth, seeing himself in the mirror above the taps as he brushed, drying his hands on the towel that hung on a rail slung below the sink. He checked the room door was locked and put the chain on, then lay down on his bed to whisper his prayers for his mum and dad, for those in need. He dozed and finally slept.

He dreamt he was walking through a forest. At first it was green and full of life, but as he walked the trees became bare and twisted and the thick vegetation was replaced by dark soil and broken rock. In front of him he saw an army marching through the desolate landscape, the feet of the soldiers pounding the ground with an incessant beat. Then the sound changed and, half-waking, he realised that someone was knocking on his door. At first, he thought it must be Devon or Jamie winding him up, like they always did after their nights on the town. There was no light in the room. The unsettled feeling he had had at Bill and Susanne's came over him again. A louder knock, and he had to get up, prank or not. He flicked on the un-shaded beam of the angle-poise and winced against the glare. The knock came a third time, and he unhooked the chain and pulled open the door. Perkins – the porter – was waiting there, blank faced. Next to him stood a female police officer and a third woman in a dark coat who looked as if she'd been woken up to be there.

"Daniel Orpheus?" The police officer asked.

"Yes."

The police officer and the other woman – she turned out to be one of the university's counsellors – came into his room, sat him down and told him that his parents were dead.

Then they took him down to the porter's lodge, as if that would make some difference. In the corridor every detail of the passage was picked out under the fluorescent strip lights: the chipped magnolia paint on the plasterboard walls, the scuffmarks on the linoleum where the fire-door scraped every time it opened. The sound of their feet on the metal stairs reverberated in the early morning stillness of the hall, and then they were walking along the narrow concrete path that led to the porter's lodge, their breath misting the night air, silhouettes of the alders by the lake picked out by the lights of the student's union beyond.

Inside the lodge he sat beside a desk on which a copy of the Daily Star lay open. On the wall in front of him was a pin-board covered with leaflets, a postcard from Ibiza showing a beach frilled by white breakers and a turquoise sea, the sand dotted with browned sunbathers. He noticed that the blue sky of the photo had faded to an odd green colour in a strip where the sun must come in each morning through the high window in the opposite wall. They bought him a cup of tea and in response to his silence the facts were amassed for his inspection. There had been a motorway pile-up – a lorry jack-knifing on black ice, then a fire. They would not have suffered – the impact was sudden. Nobody to blame.

Chapter 2

The woods were dark around him, the rock cold at his back. He watched the fish cook. His body was at rest but in his mind was restless. His thoughts went back a few days, to the incident that showed how strongly his urge to move was influencing him. He'd tried to kill a boar – a much more substantial prize than the rabbits and fish he usually lived off. He had had salt in his pack still, enough to cure the meat. If he had been intending to stay in the forest it would have made no sense to salt meat in the spring, using his last reserves well before the winter – but, for a journey, having salted meat was a good plan. The idea was rational once he accepted the irrational impulse to move. He'd known that a boar would provide far more meat than he needed but that couldn't be helped; the crows and the foxes would finish the rest.

He'd reconnoitred the woods, finding the places where the boars were active, where the ground was dug up and churned over as they foraged for roots and tubers. Choosing a spot close to the most recent rooting places, where a collapsed badger sett made a hollow that helped his purpose, he'd taken out his fold-away spade and dug out a steep-sided pit. The ground had been soft and, in an hour or so, he'd had the basis of his trap. He'd found a fallen branch thin enough to cut with his knife, sliced it into three stakes, sharpened at one end, and dug them into the base of the pit. He'd used light branches, bracken, moss and mulch to create a fragile roof that would make the trap practically invisible. Finally, he'd dug up some bulbs and roots himself, and thrown them onto the flimsy covering.

'Our Father, who art in heaven…' he whispered the words aloud, into the darkness of his room.

There's nobody there, is there?

'Hallowed be thy name'

What sort of God would let this happen?

'Thy kingdom come; thy will be done.'

Where was that pan his mum had bought him as a going away present? His voice faltered.

'On earth as it is in heaven'

What reason could He have for it?

She'd wanted to know what he'd been making himself to eat.

'Give us this day our daily bread, and forgive us our trespasses'

He should ask you to forgive Him.

'As we forgive those who trespass against us'

They're dead.

'And lead us not into temptation, but deliver us from evil'

I didn't even speak to them last week.

Too busy with Bill and Susanne.

I've got no home.

New wine, new skins.

The next day frost crystals adorned every blade of grass, every branch. There was silence and stillness. He watched it through his bedroom window. From his cocoon. His thoughts, fragmented and unbound, searched for a new pattern. He picked up his bible, but now the words only brought him back to his pain. At around ten he heard whispers in the corridor, a soft knock. So, they knew – Devon, Jamie, Sarah. Jane. Knew that while they were out drinking his parents had been killed. He ignored the knocking, stayed silent and as still as the frost-sparkled trees outside.

He did not keep track of the passing morning and he kept his mobile turned off. Eventually there was a firmer knock on the door, and he heard Bill's voice through the thin wood.

"Daniel, its Bill and Susanne. I know you're their old chap. Will you let us in?"

Mechanically, he stood up and unlocked the door, and Bill opened it from the outside. He sat down again, avoiding a hug from Susanne, who sat next to him on the bed instead. Bill pulled the chair over from the desk.

"Oh Daniel ..." Susanne put her arm around him. There was a long silence. There did not seem to be anything for anyone to say. Bill broke it, eventually, practically –

"Daniel, you can't stay here. You can come back to our place – we've got two spare rooms and you won't be disturbed. You won't need to worry about anything."

"No, of course not. God will take care of it."

"Daniel ..." Susanne tried to speak, but he stood up and broke her hold.

"This was 'meant to be', I suppose?" Suddenly he wanted to be with people who enjoyed life while they could. The people he had been avoiding all this time. "I have my room here. I'm sorry."

He walked to the window and stared out so he didn't have to see them anymore, could ignore their mumbled attempts to change his mind. He stood firm against the voice inside that wanted him to be nice to them, to make them happy, to go back to how it was. Because it wasn't that way anymore.

$$*$$

"Why weren't you interested?" Jane hesitated. "Before?"

They still walked on eggshells with him a bit, even six months later. Maybe that's why she'd let him – well it didn't matter. She was pressed close to him in her single bed.

"I was. But I thought I shouldn't. You know, religion and all that."

"You believed in it though."

"I know. It's not so obvious from inside."

"What?"

"How you're being controlled. You don't even see it. Neither do they – they don't understand what they're doing. Look at Bill and Susanne." He shuddered.

"The Dean? He seems OK though."

"They all seem 'OK'. They're not sinister, not really. Just misguided. But in a way that screws people up. Makes you think it's wrong to want anything," he squeezed her. "Anything physical anyway."

"But now it doesn't worry you? Well," she giggled. "Obviously it doesn't."

"And you were here to take advantage of my fall." She'd been the first to, at least. They kissed. And if he went out and didn't pull he could always knock on her door and get a welcome.

"*I thought I shouldn't.*" That came back to him later as he sat at the little study desk in his room trying to write an assignment. Fine to think of Bill and Susanne saying that – or thinking it. But that his parents would have thought it – that was something different. He wished Jane and the others would stop referring to it.

So, think about it. Reason it out. Why do you feel guilty? What purpose does it have?

This was the tool he'd found to make sense of everything. The tool Pemberton had been holding out all the time. The logic of selection, the reason behind it all. This was what had set him free. The method. There was an answer to everything if you had the mental discipline to find it. So, what was the evolutionary purpose of guilt? He stared out of the window over the willow trees and the grey blocks of the other halls. It was about relationships, obviously – you felt guilty about how you had affected another person, or other people. Beyond sexual partnership though – guilt was wider than that. Friendly relationships could be beneficial for survival because of the extra support each person got if they had problems – especially if the people involved had complementary skills. There would be an issue of trust though. It might be best to get help from those around you and avoid giving it back. Except others might notice that, and then you wouldn't get help any more. No, hold on – he chewed his pen. That was it – if there was an *instinct* that stopped you cheating or made you want to make up for it, then you would in general behave more trustworthily. And then you would have more support when you needed it. Guilt could have a fitness value. The problem would be that if a bond broke for some other reason, that instinct couldn't just switch off in that same instant. You would have the effects of it even after it stopped being useful. You would feel guilty at going against the other person even when it didn't matter anymore. He rocked back in his chair with relief. That meant there was no value in the loyalty his guilt wanted him to show, because his parents were dead. Those feelings were no longer useful. He could ignore them. He should ignore them.

There you go – straightforward.

There really was always an answer if you followed the logic. No wooliness, just discipline. And release. Three hours later, he wandered into the shared kitchen with a confidence that the others had got used to over the past few weeks. The awkwardness of death had been buried quickly – Daniel had insisted on it.

"The task in hand gentleman," he said as he took a seat at the grimy table. "Is to plan our strategy for the evening."

"Do you ever not have a plan?" Devon swigged his beer.

"No, he always has a plan," chimed in Jamie. Another guy from

24

the next block – Mark – sat in the corner staring at his phone and apparently ignoring them.

"And do they work?" Daniel countered.

"For you they do."

"Well, sometimes for me too," Devon laughed. "Go on then, what is it tonight? The Flag and then Wired?"

"Yeah, there's a promotion on in The Flag."

"That's true Jamie," Daniel agreed. "But I was thinking more of The Boatman – it's sunny – riverside garden, girls in summer dresses…"

"And Jane'll be in The Flag and you fancy a change."

Daniel swigged from a small bottle of expensive Spanish lager, but not too deeply. "No Devon, nothing to do with …"

But he was drowned out by jeers – even Mark joined in. That was fine – here – but he made sure he never said anything to fuel it. And he was pretty sure they wouldn't spread it further – his straightforward approach had got them girls too, so they had no interest in spoiling things. And they were a bit afraid to upset him, given what had happened.

"Anyway, what the fuck was Steve up to this morning?" The others followed Devon down a rambling trail of half-cut conversational flow, tumbling from subject to subject, Daniel watching and playing his part. Later, on the lawn by the river, another bottle in hand – this one the type that comes with a lemon jammed in the top – he got talking to some tipsy girls with wide, open smiles, and the night flowed as easily as the chatter. One of them kept looking at him and he kept looking back – a tall, slim blonde with wide-set brown eyes that he could stare into and get lost. They danced together in Wired, moving ever nearer to each other until he pulled her close and she laughed, and they kissed. At last, for a while, there was no space for anything else in his mind.

"Why don't you take me somewhere more private?" She

whispered between kisses.

"Sounds good."

As they were leaving, she leaning against him because of the booze, he caught the eye of Giles, propping up a pillar at the edge of the dance floor. Daniel nodded to him without going over. Giles was a player – girls and rugby. What did that glance mean? The last thing he wanted was people taking notice of him, spreading gossip.

He found out soon enough what it meant, next day at lunchtime as he sat yawning in the college canteen with a sandwich and a coffee. The 'lads' weren't up yet – he'd lost them on the dancefloor and had no idea where they'd ended up – their messages hadn't made much sense. He was trying to read 'Science' – it was always his starter for the day – then into the heavier stuff. Giles came and sat next to him so that they looked out side by side over the table, the rest of the café, the grass and trees outside the windows. Did he think he was in a spy film or something?

"What can I do for you Giles?"

"Just thought I'd say hello."

"No, you didn't. Good night last night?"

"No better than yours I would say." He grinned.

"That's my business."

"OK, OK, no need to be uptight. But I'm curious. From what Devon says ..."

"Don't believe everything Devon tells you – he's off his face most of the time."

"– You've got Jane wrapped around your finger. But that blonde last night, she was something."

"Like I said, that's my business. Anyway, she just needed someone to walk her home."

"She just needed something, and my bet is you gave it her. No, wait a sec. I'm just curious how you do it. Different one every night more or less…"

"You're jumping to conclusions Giles."

"I don't think so. Listen, I do pretty well myself but there's always room to improve – and you've got more plates spinning than a – plate spinner. People like us need to stick together."

"People like us? I don't know what you mean."

But he was right – they did need to stick together in one sense – if Giles chose to spread around what he'd seen, his social life might get much trickier. But Giles was a rugby player, and he had his rules – never leave your wing man, your mates are more valuable than some girl, that kind of thing. He would stick to his word, more or less. So, strategically –

"Well, you might be right about me, and you might not. Everyone knows your game, but they don't know mine, and I don't really want them to. So, if you want me to share what I know that's fine – and I won't step on your toes if you know what I mean. But respect my privacy. Deal?"

"Deal." They shook on it.

"There's no real secret," said Daniel. "Just two simple things: one, be straightforward. Ask straight out for what you want or go straight for it. If they don't like it, they'll tell you – probably feel flattered – in that case, don't dwell on it, move on. Anyway, you know that. It's the logic of nature – forget all the social nonsense we layer on top of it. Second: discipline. I've heard you talking about your girls – across the room sometimes. You're talking and everyone's listening and then they go away and get drunk and mention something and before you know it your cover's blown or your reputation. Or you post stuff online and everyone gets to know that way. Girls see you coming."

"Half the fun's talking about it though, isn't it?"

"But only half – if that. How much of the actual thing is worth giving up for the benefit of telling the story? I don't mean never speak and never post anything. But choose what you say and to whom. Do what the politicians do – a bit of spin. You do it anyway, but think about why – what impression are you giving? What good does that do you? And if you keep your mouth shut and someone else is talking and you're listening, then you're the one learning. Think about the girls too – they talk to each other you know. That means you've got to be careful again – what you do and how. Sometimes that might mean letting them know things – always good to show you're experienced. But control it."

"You think everything out like that?"

"Those plates don't spin themselves."

Giles stared at him for a moment. "You're a cold bastard aren't you?" He stood up. "I was thinking when I came over – maybe we could be a team; pool resources and all that. But I think I've changed my mind. A deal's a deal though – I'll steer clear of you and I won't say anything."

It was bullshit, the steering clear part – if Giles wanted a girl, he'd get her. But the other part he believed, and that was the important bit. More scruples than expected though. Amazing how many rules even people like him had – internal stories that didn't really amount to doing anything differently. But sitting there on his own with his coffee he couldn't raise even an inner smile about his superior approach. He went over the logic again and pressed down his rising sense of guilt once more.

*

Bob Pemberton had a problem; a PhD student 'finishing' before she had finished had left him with a financial headache and a paper short of what was expected from him for annual reporting – his teaching load and administration meant he couldn't write them himself anymore. He had other students, but they were over busy with what they already had to work on, and his post docs didn't

28

quite fit the subject. When he was a student he'd watched professors be allowed to gently fade into a haze of theory and pipe smoke, sunny afternoons and beer, anecdotes and respect, unbothered after the toil of their earlier years. They were still somehow present on quiet corridors and in odd corners of the college library. Not for him – not with publication recording and funding cuts and accountancy and the hideous shadow of 'growing the student experience'. Even when one was really too old, novel research had to spawn papers apace, interactive teaching was required, a form of instruction that, unlike the old form, could not be allowed to drift into leaning on a lectern and propounding whatever theory occurred to you, until the phalanx of faces in front had slackened into torpor.

Anyway, his student had done most of her fieldwork and had been halfway through transcribing the figures from the hand-written data sheets. She'd had a conference paper under her belt, not to mention a near perfect academic record. Such a waste to walk away. Anyway, not worth worrying about now. The question was, who was her replacement? He could advertise but the admin process was labyrinthine. What about the third years? They were doing their exams now, so someone keen might be dragged straight in once they'd finished. Might even be able to use the same grant money if he pulled some strings.

He reached down a pile of files from the end of a shelf, and for once they were the ones he needed, as if they had been logically filed and he the assiduous archivist. His colleagues had all this stuff on files on their PCs but he couldn't quite let go of the old ways. Janet Sanders: odds on first, but she had a plan involving horses and homeopathy – great for Geoff and equine science but no interest in the evolution of tropical plants. He shuffled through a mixed bag of 2:1's. Here were some more firsts: Peter Etherington – good but no imagination somehow. He didn't want a technician, although knowing new methods seemed more important today than being able to think. And Daniel Orpheus. Now he was an interesting one. Distinctly hostile in the first year – under Bill Peter's wing he'd heard – until his parents died. Then a week after that knocking on his door and taking away a list of references as long as his arm, and – if his assignments were anything to go by – actually finding and reading them. All those surly religious references disappeared and off he went. OK, from his questions he seemed most interested in human behaviour and its evolution, rather than plants – but he was engaged with the other topics too and his logic was usually spot on. Peter was no comparison, imagination wise, and thinking of papers Daniel had a good writing style. Yes – he stretched – of that lot he was the best and as far as he knew no-one else had their claws in him. Rays of evening sunshine trickled into his office through the window behind him, softened and filtered by the great tree out there on the grass. He packed some papers into his satchel and headed for home.

Chapter 3

"We know the questions we need to address next, and we know the answer lie here." The screen behind Daniel glowed green with a full slide photo of verdant rainforest. He looked around at his colleagues, representing skills and expertise complementary to his own. Some of them were senior to him but, none of them had risen as fast as he had. What was it? Three years since he'd finished the PhD under Pemberton? Not so hard really once you had a clear mind.

"As you will be aware," he continued. "The samples returned from the last research trip were revealing but raised questions which will require new funding and new, cutting-edge techniques to deliver. We're a small team at the moment, but the good news is, that our work has bought us some attention."

The screen switched to a swirling logo that cleverly blended natural and geometric shapes, the letters 'OPE' emerging satisfyingly from the design.

"One Planet Enterprises – you've heard of them of course – leaders in the development of pharmaceutical products from natural compounds."

He reeled off figures on turnover, number of employees, international reach, his grey eyes switching between the members of his small audience, expertly keeping them engaged. The shyness of the student Daniel was gone, his somewhat gaunt form could now be described as sporty, his suit was expensive and his tie a shade of green that matched the hues of the rainforest and the OPE logo.

"In the past, we've looked to our national research bodies and international organisations for funding. The commercial sector brings another level of opportunity. These are the big players – Oxford, Cambridge, York have led the way in developing private collaborations at a strategic level – if we want to keep up, we have to do the same, and OPE can put us in that game." Then he ran through the research proposal, his narrative clipped and to-the-point. "What I would like today, is your approval in moving forward with this plan." He sat down at the head of the oval table and looked around.

On the other side of the triple glazed windows, morning sunlight splashed over the rolling lawn of the college grounds. Rooks strutted, occasionally pausing to jab down into the grass, pulling out soft white crane-fly larvae and swallowing them down, leaving a little eruption of dark soil on the manicured sward. The sound of their relaxed caws bounced off the windowpanes unheard. Within there was only the hum of air-conditioning behind the voices, a dry stillness of carpet and glass and steel and laptop screens and fake leather chairs and disposable coffee cups. The conversation crept on and took the whole of Daniel's attention.

"I'm struggling with the samples we're being sent – I really need to get out there and direct things. If we can get OPE in and they can bring the funds we need, I'm all for it." That was Frank Jones, a small, energetic man who Daniel knew felt constrained by his current lack of resources.

"But," asked Frank. "What's the level of OPE's interest? Are they really likely to buy into this?"

"I spoke to their CEO, Lord Denver, at the last conference in London. He's a very impressive man, dynamic, open to new ideas. The New Guinea rainforest area has been a focus for them for some time, as a source of new materials, especially for medicinal use. But they're having trouble on the ground – they don't have many connections in the local area, and the government is, as you know, cagey about who gets access to what."

"But we have those connections," nodded Frank. "If they came in with us ..."

"They would be on the inside track. And for us, as well as the direct funding, there would be opportunities to build joint capacity on the molecular front, and to further our evolutionary studies. They've seen what being associated with major scientific breakthroughs can do for corporate image."

"What are we looking at then? In terms of scale?" Asked Jill.

If there had not been a ceiling above them, they could have looked up into white-grey billows of cloud, beneath which swirling flock of swifts cut the air with acrobatic turns: slim, dark crescents diving and soaring with high-pitched cries, aware of air currents and moisture and light, of movement, of constant change. The meeting moved towards a conclusion.

"The big question is," said Frank, leaning forward. "Do you think the New Guinean government will be happy with it?"

"Just what I wanted to ask you, Frank," Daniel shot back. "You know them best – how do we sell it to them?"

"Hmm." The older man paused for a moment. "I think we keep emphasizing the university research element and play down the corporate stuff. If we include them as a partner, they would go for it. I'm sure OPE have a team capable of ensuring that they can make the most of the opportunity, once we've got them in."

"Good, then what – "

"Sorry to interrupt."

Daniel stopped – it was the post-doc – what was his name? Anthony? Invited because of his research interest in Papua New Guinea – someone had thought it was a good idea, although he wasn't senior enough to have a real influence.

"But, weren't OPE involved in that scandal in Brazil – the 'disappeared forest'? Do we really want to be linked to them?"

Yes, it was true OPE hadn't come out of that affair well but, what multi-national hadn't mis-stepped?

"Lord Denver is across the issues in a way his predecessor really wasn't – although keep that to yourselves – OPE need to embrace the sustainability agenda like anyone else. If we don't work with them, others will, and we'll be left behind. It's naïve to think otherwise I'm afraid. There's a lot of new material out there Anthony – have a read of it. OPE have moved on from the old days, and we have to help them do more. Lord Denver is one of the good guys."

"But isn't there a conflict of interest in us presenting this work as independent university research when it's basically a commercial venture?"

Jill answered for him. "Anthony, there are institutes who would give their right arm for this kind of opportunity. If we don't take it, OPE will just go to somebody else."

"And the returns for all the work we've done so far will go to somebody else too." That was Frank. Good, he had the ones that counted onside. If he pulled this off and could get the trust of OPE, he would be a cert for the chair and a lot more besides. Outside one of the rooks tore a particularly fat, writhing worm out of the earth, its dark eyes gleaming.

✳

The next day, Pemberton sat in his office, papers stacked on his desk left and right of him, and indeed stacked on every flat surface as well as the parts of the floor he didn't need to walk on. To get around his desk he had to duck beneath the fronds of a large-leaved tropical plant that was threatening to take over. He was reading with an increasingly heavy heart Daniel's precisely worded report on the strategic partnership with OPE. The text and the presentation were immaculate; he had known they would be. And so was the logic, the cold rationality. Self-interest distilled, mixed with knowledge, wedded to opportunity and spelt out. Of course, he'd seen writing of Daniel's like this before – but in theoretical papers where that principle cut away the thickets of waffle. Natural selection – the single logical underpinning of nature and humanity. What he himself taught. But this was a real proposal – something that could have serious consequences. OPE he knew of old; as a young idealist he'd protested against them on more than one occasion. Had even spent a night in the cells. And Denver – he'd run into him a few times since and expended a fair amount of effort stopping him from gaining a toehold in research. Blast Daniel for putting him in this position. The department head would take a dim view of turning down a chance like this – but to support it, to be associated with it…

He stood up and turned to stare out of his window at a rolling lawn still blue-grey with dew, the dark graceful shape of the Cedar of Lebanon that shaded his office on hot summer days, so that he had to use a special lamp to keep his plants healthy, that more seriously threatened the foundations of the building. But he wouldn't want to cut it down. He made himself think. Daniel had taken all the theory and applied it as it was – no softening of it, no bloody common sense. He sighed. Of course he had, you idiot. After his parents. He sat down, leant back in his chair, and ran his hands through what remained of his hair. How could he sort this one out?

Over dinner with his wife that evening, he was uncharacteristically quiet. He could tell that Caroline noticed, but she left it until after they'd eaten, both settling down on the sofa in the lamplit front room. "So, what's keeping that great brain occupied this evening?"

"Ha. Daniel Orpheus."

"Your post-doc? The one whose –?"

"Parents died. Yes, that's the one."

"I thought he was doing really well – 'filling the coffers.'"

"Oh, he's doing that alright. We'll be taking on staff before long, making the papers I wouldn't doubt."

"Which is why you took him on of course."

"Yes, it is."

"So?"

"So. OPE. So, Lord Denver." He poured himself some more wine.

"Go on."

"He's been talking to them. More than talking – planning. I knew they were trying to get into the research game. Some kind of fig leaf I suppose."

"Not much of one."

"If you want to believe enough… Anyway – can you pass me another one of those chocolates?"

"The last strawberry one?"

"If you insist darling. Thanks. You know, I never really made that bit of my past public – the protest stuff."

"I know."

"Maybe you were right about that being a mistake." He looked away to avoid her smile. "If he'd known he might not have – anyway, he has."

"Can't you just warn him off?"

"I think he may have pinned rather a lot on this."

"And you didn't know?"

"You know how it is."

"How it was with that other post doc – David – you mean? How it was with, what was her name? The one whose PhD Daniel took over?"

"Claire. You don't have to – I realise. It's just …"

"I'm sorry," she put an arm round him. "I know it's not easy. But if you don't keep track of them …"

He sighed. "Actually, it's worse than that, I think."

"You always have liked – what's the new phrase? – 'super-wicked problems'. Worse how?"

"I was thinking back to when I took him on. I'd always wondered about that change – when his parents died, you know – from hating every word I said to not being able to get enough."

"I remember. It was a reaction, of course. You were worried it might just be a passing interest – that he would throw it all up."

"Yes."

"And now?"

"And now I've read his report and read back over some of his other work. And, well, I think the problem might be the opposite. I think he believes in it. I mean, not like believing a theory, I mean ..."

"Like a faith."

"It's not funny."

"I didn't laugh."

"Survival of the fittest is a bloody concept, not a blueprint for living your life."

"He's being logically consistent."

"He's not even got the theory straight – you don't have to literally be self-interested all the time."

"I've seen you dancing on a pinhead before dear – no need to do it again."

"But it's vital – being altruistic or caring about people isn't ruled out ..."

"As I said, no need to tell me. But I do think you're being a bit arrogant."

"What? How? I'm just stating the facts – he's obviously somehow made a very basic mistake."

"That's what I mean – has he? Or is he just following the argument to its conclusion – i.e., farther than you would like to?"

"Not this again."

Over the years it had been a running joke of hers to point out to him each occasion his choices failed to be in his rational self-interest, and a game of his to find an evolutionary explanation. The next day she would always send him to work with his lunch in a battered old tin of 'Ye Olde Devonshire Clotted Cream Fudge' to get the last word.

"No, listen. He's acting on what you taught him. All our desires evolved, so they line up with what's in our best interests."

"Don't try that one – they were in our best interests once, when they evolved. But the modern world is different – they don't necessarily align now."

"Quite. And if they don't, presumably it might be a superior tactic to ignore them – to follow what we work out is best for us and ignore our feelings."

"I don't think –"

"Sometimes you don't want to dear. Daniel's worked out what he thinks is the best strategy for success. And given that's the logic behind all our other instincts anyway, even altruism and empathy – and love as you're so fond of mentioning – then there's nothing wrong with ignoring them is there? Not if your motive for doing that is the same motive those things evolved to give you."

"It's not that simple."

"You mean it makes it sound too much like psychopathy?"

"Oh come on – you're saying he's a psycho now? Really?"

"Not clinically – well who knows but that's not what I mean. I think his brain is probably as normal as anyone else's if that means anything. What I mean is, the logical conclusion of following your ideas is for someone who wants success to behave like he's doing.

And he's doing OK, isn't he? Ignoring instincts that don't line up with self-interest anymore. Burying any feeling that tells him that's not right."

"It's not that ..."

"Simple – so you said. Look Bob, you've got to face up to this. If you don't believe it – not really, not enough to live by it yourself – don't say it. Or at least, make it a bit softer – admit the possibility of something more."

"No money in soft. No papers."

"No papers! Don't start trying it yourself or if you do, go the whole way and take the OPE money. Makes sense, doesn't it? If that comes in while you're head of research ..."

"– I'd never forgive myself."

"– You'll be made as much as Daniel will be. And he knows you can work that out – so he'll expect your support."

"What can I do though? Reject it? How would that look?"

"If you're thinking that way, I can't help I'm afraid. Read your book, I've got the crossword to do."

She grabbed the paper and shifted into the armchair, and he couldn't get any more from her.

The next day when she handed him his lunchbox, he looked down expectantly, only to see a plain Tuppaware box.

"Sorry Bob, this is serious. It's about Daniel's life, not yours. You have to put it right. Not OPE and Denver and all that – what he believes."

Chapter 4

That night he'd stayed in the open, close to the trap; he'd not wanted to disturb the boar but the squeals of an injured animal could attract unwanted attention if not quickly silenced. He'd slept little, flushed with adrenalin at the thought of the kill. Like the thrill of killing the thief. Sometimes it was as if that horror had happened hours, not months, before. Time had passed, the sky lightening, and he had started to regret the effort of digging and covering the pit, when the shrieks he had been waiting for had jolted him from his half-sleep. He'd sprinted the few metres to the hole, felt the cold dampness of the new day fresh on his face, the familiar shape of his knife handle, comfortable in his hand. Reaching the trap, it had been obvious that a boar was caught – the meshed vegetation of the 'roof' had been caved in and the sounds of the struggling animal disrupted the melodies of the dawn chorus. But his plan had not been completely fulfilled; somehow the animal had managed to avoid being impaled by the sharpened stakes. She had still been trapped though, confined tightly between two of the stakes and the earth wall of her prison.

*

"– And don't drink too much," Daniel added.

Kate – his girlfriend for how long? Two years now? – didn't reply. He stepped ahead of her and pressed the doorbell. He was edgy. Strange to think that a few years ago this place had seemed like a refuge. Now, coming here was just an awkward social necessity. The windows of the house glowed, projecting the atmosphere of the party, and they shuffled on the step, wind whipping a drizzle of rain around them, unseasonably cold for early September. Eventually Bill came to the door.

"Good evening." The frostiness in his voice was levelled at

Daniel. More gently and with a smile he turned to Kate. "Kate, lovely to see you, how are you?"

"Good thanks – busy. We've been looking forward to the party."

Daniel walked past them into the house, the Dean having taken his coat. He had been unable to avoid introducing Kate to Bill and Susanne, and she'd developed a real friendship with them. She was a physical geographer and as fate would have it, Bill had studied geography as an undergraduate. Daniel straightened the cuffs of his dress shirt and looked around the room. He knew it, but not well – apart from the piano room he had hardly been in the 'public' parts of the house. He remembered those Sunday teas in the back parlour. Those civilised, pathetic lunches. This room was for formal parties, and as an undergraduate he had never felt comfortable at those. It was large, high-ceilinged, with ornate, overbearing furniture pressed back towards the walls.

The cleared space in the middle of the room accommodated a gaggle of academics gathered under the light of an elaborate chandelier. Most of the guests had been there an hour already, and were talking freely, increasingly under the spell of the Rioja supplied by Susanne. She wore a glittering blue dress, moving easily between the conversational groups into which the party had divided. With his scientific mind, he saw her influence forming them into a kind of meta-population in which the death of one conversation could be compensated for by the spread of another.

Many of the guests he didn't know and wasn't interested in. Hangers-on and climbers – he saw it in the eagerness of their eyes as they spoke to the more senior professors, their uncomfortable body language. There was Chambers, the hawk-faced departmental head and his angular wife, and Pemberton– the closest person to a friend in the room – short, bespectacled, his thinning grey hair defiantly adrift above the precision of his formal dress. Daniel hadn't spoken to him for a couple of days – he would have to make sure his OPE report wasn't buried in one of those infamous paper stacks.

Who else was there? He picked out a couple of visitors he had expected; one of them was Sloan, a complete bore who, unsurprisingly alone, was gazing balefully around the room. Daniel looked quickly away to avoid catching his eye. By the fireplace he saw a petite blonde sipping a glass of wine. She wore a low-cut, flowery dress and he couldn't help noticing how it brought out the curves of her body. He realised that he recognised her: a couple of days ago, having his morning coffee in the refectory, he had looked up from his paper and caught her staring at him with a look that had completely derailed his train of thought. Perhaps there would be some excitement tonight after all. But now Kate and Peters caught up with him, and Susanne materialised from nowhere and pressed a glass of red into his hand –

"Daniel, Kate, glad you could make it! It's great so many people have turned up on such a miserable night." She must have hoped that the vice chancellor would come. He allowed his glance to rest on flowery-dress girl. Kate filled in the gap in the conversation.

"Well, it's been so long since we've seen you – Bill was just telling me you'd been ill."

"Yes, some dreadful flu virus – Bill always comes down with that sort of thing at the start of a new term, then I get it three times worse."

Still soldiering on though.

The girl was gazing at the oil painting that hung over the fireplace. It was a sweeping landscape: a shepherd drove his flock along a track in the foreground to the left, and a wide plain opened out behind, speckled with trees, a river, an indistinct town whose featureless spread was punctuated by the abrupt point of a church steeple. A blue haze of low, rounded hills occupied the far horizon. His eye was drawn to the group of huntsmen on horseback to the right of the scene, careering down a slope towards a beech wood, the white smears of the hounds in full cry ahead of them, the leader in his scarlet coat raising a horn to his lips, and in front of them all the burnished form of the fox. Although the animal was little more than a smudge of paint, Daniel sensed rather than saw its head turned back to stare fearfully at its pursuers. One couldn't tell if the fox's pace would be fast enough for it to reach the safety of the trees or whether it would be brought to ground beneath the towering white clouds that blossomed against a blue sky.

For some reason Daniel found the tableau so intensely unsettling that he forgot his plan to use their mutual interest in the painting as a pre-text to talk to the girl. Stupid to be upset by it – looking more intently he saw how awkwardly painted the figures on the horses were – only the colours of the sky showed any skill in the brush work. And yet…

He turned back to Kate and Susanne, resigning himself to the flat domestic exchange. But the Dean's wife had noticed the drifting of his attention and punished him for it:

"You must meet Professor Sloan – he's just published a fascinating paper in 'Proceedings' – Professor Sloan!"

The Professor smiled at them, bespectacled, precise.

"This is Daniel Orpheus, a current star of the department." Sloan looked as if the almost empty glass of wine he held had been his limit. "And this is Kate, from Geography."

Handshakes all round. "I'm sure you'll want to talk."

Almost without pause, Sloan began a monologue on spiders. But Susanne's revenge missed its target: Kate, who made the mistake of showing interest in the professor's topic, became the focus of his attentions, while Daniel caught Chambers' eye – he and his group were next to them – and started to talk to him.

In the way that often happens at parties, Daniel, Chambers and his entourage drifted and were separated from Sloan and Kate without anyone being conscious of moving. This gentle choreography took Daniel with a seeming inevitability towards the girl in the flowery dress. She was talking to another woman, older than her; severe looking. Chambers, noticing the direction of Daniel's glance, made some introductions.

"Daniel, have you met Sophie Hayes? – she's working over in Paleontology."

No, he hadn't, but was delighted to. Her eyes were refreshingly unguarded; she wasn't wearing make-up and her long blonde hair flowed over her shoulders.

"Sophie, this is Dr Daniel Orpheus, one of our most talented evolutionary biologists."

Her hand was small and warm, squeezing his. Their eyes met for just a little longer than was polite before Daniel took the hand of the older woman, another palaeontologist whose name he forgot even as she was saying it. Perhaps aware of those little things, she turned to talk to Chambers and he and Sophie were left together, the others in the group faithfully following the conversation of the more senior man.

"So, Sophie, how did you get into palaeontology?"

It was a dull question but that didn't matter. He looked at her with such direct and open desire that she smiled and blushed, started to look away – but didn't. She answered – something. He replied. The ball was hit to and fro, but the game was just a side show continued for the benefit of their company. Everything they really wanted to say was exchanged in a long penetrating gaze that left no question for either of them. He used to be frightened to really look at girls that way, until he realised what it could do – the boldness of an unbroken stare and the soft nothingness of conversation, the accompanying music to the dance; the dance of fighting fish in courtship, of ravens intertwining in flight. Nothing sentimental – just instinct. They stayed like that, their voices weaving around one another for a few minutes, no more. Then the gentle push, the next step –

"Where do you live?"

"I've got a flat around the corner, on Cheltenham Road – Belvedere Gardens." A pause, a glance up at him and a smile. "Would you like to see it?"

"I would, very much," he looked around them. "But perhaps you should go ahead, and I can join you there in a bit?" He could see the excitement of the little deception build inside her as he spoke. She tipped back the last of her wine without taking her eyes off him.

"Flat 12." She walked past him towards the door, and he turned and watched her for a second, the sway of her hips. Looking up he caught Bill staring across at him. Had the Dean seen the lust in his glance? Well, what did it matter? Daniel nodded curtly to him and turned to Pemberton, who was in discussion with a couple of under-grads by the window. As the professor noticed him it seemed to Daniel that his expression clouded for a second –

"Daniel! How are you?"

"I'm good, thanks." The under grads looked serious and edgy.

"I was just talking to Paul and David here about drug resistance – there's a new paper out in Nature."

"Holden?"

"Yes."

"The Red Queen in action." The two students looked at him blankly. Where did they get these people from?

"You must have heard of van Valen?" He could see they hadn't. "Alice in Wonderland? The Red Queen runs to stay still – antibiotics put a selection pressure on a disease to evolve. When it does you have to change the drug just to keep having the same impact."

They nodded in unison

"You need to start thinking about behavioural patterns in terms of individual self-interest. Because even when organisms look like they're cooperating, their interests won't be quite the same. And then you get those evolutionary contests. That's almost certainly the reason we've got such large brains – even if we don't use much of them." He smiled at his own coded put-down but Pemberton didn't seem to have noticed it. The students gazed at him expectantly and he plunged on –

"Women value different things to men – their instincts evolved to increase their chances of conceiving with the fittest man and to having their offspring cared for by the best parent. Men's interests on the other hand are to spread their genes as widely as possible, and to make sure they don't end up parenting someone else's children because their wife's been cheating. So, it's an arms race between sexes: women get better at finding ways to secure the best man, men get better at pretending to be the best man and spreading those genes."

"But what about love?" Was that Paul, or David? – He couldn't remember –

"Love! Ha! How romantic of you. The love meme is just a great way to keep your partner close – say 'I love you' and you look committed and faithful. Then she'll be more likely to stay. But you still have to watch out – she might stay with you, but whose kids does she really want to have?" He thought Pemberton's smile seemed a bit fixed, but he carried on. The professor must have had too much wine as well.

"It's all a sub-conscious game. All this politeness is a sham," he waved his arm around the room. "It's all a competition – if you want to do well, you're going to have to read more and know more than the next man – or woman."

Pleased though he was to hold these slightly intimidated students in thrall, Daniel was conscious that he had an appointment to keep.

"Anyway – I'm sorry, I've got to go I'm afraid – some papers to finish tonight – we've all got to keep running!"

But Pemberton's voice held him back for a moment "You and Kate must join us for dinner next week."

Taken off guard, Daniel agreed. If he had been more attentive, he wouldn't have – although he respected the professor theirs was not a close relationship, and he'd never met his wife, who he'd heard disliked these formal parties. It would be awkward, over-polite, and

Kate would be charming, and they would say what a lovely couple they were – all of that. But the arrangement was made now.

Finally edging away, he strode over to Kate, who was still in Sloan's clutches. Susanne might have saved her, but she was deep in conversation with Sophie's palaeontologist friend and hadn't noticed her predicament. In comparison with Sophie's quick smile and bright eyes Daniel thought Kate's face looked tired, over-serious: the lines around her mouth, the furrow of her brow seemed accentuated.

"Kate, I'm sorry – Pemberton's just reminded me of some papers that need going through back at the office – it'll only take a couple of hours, but it'll save us a lot of trouble tomorrow. You don't mind?"

With Sloan there she didn't have many socially acceptable options for honesty and so, no, she didn't mind. Leaving her with a kiss on the cheek Daniel made for the door. If he could just make it past Bill – but, no, inevitably the Dean broke off from his conversation, intercepting Daniel before he could make his escape. "A word Daniel?"

Like Susanne – always meddling. Daniel followed his host out into the hallway. Glancing back, he caught Kate smiling after him parentally – because he was with Bill, he supposed – she would be expecting a reconciliation.

"What is it, Peters?" They had stepped out into the hall and the closing of the door cut off the buzz of the party, the classical music that ebbed and flowed in the background.

"Susanne and I are – concerned. Not just about Kate, though God knows she doesn't deserve the way you treat her. But about you as well Daniel."

Or more precisely, about my soul thought Daniel. He knew this game. He'd played it. He'd followed it more strictly even than them – the ideology ingrained in him so strongly by his parents. Bill continued –

"We understand why you changed Daniel – we think it's a mistake, we hope you'll turn back – but we understand. But this kind of thing ..." He gestured irrelevantly towards the front door. Daniel remembered when Peters and Susanne had been his closest friends. But that was then. What did they offer him now? Really, what had they ever offered? Empty fantasies that had kept him alone.

"What I do with my life is no concern of yours – not anymore."

"Kate's a friend. And so were you – once."

"Kate and I understand each other. I've never pretended to be anything other than I am."

"So, you told her where you were going? She doesn't mind?"

"Like I said, it's no concern of yours."

"If your parents could see you ..."

"Drop it, Peters. You don't know anything about it." Pulling on his coat, he dragged the door open. A flurry or rain disturbed the still warmth of the hall and he stepped out into the night.

"We'll be here for you Daniel. Whatever you do."

Daniel slammed the wrought iron garden gate behind him with a metallic clang. What right had they to offer that? He didn't ask for it. Head down against the wind he walked south west down Gloucester Street. Litter blew down the road from an overturned wheelie bin; a can of coke trundling over the tarmac, a discarded chip wrapper fluttering briefly before it stuck to the pavement. His dad used to take him to buy fish and chips when he was a kid. The shop with a gaudily coloured counter so high that he had to be lifted up to say hello to the girl frying the potatoes. He could see the cod and the sausages waiting in piles under the heaters in their golden jackets, smell the fat and the scent of tobacco from his dad's coat. They would take the hot paper packets back home to his mum and the three of them would sit round the kitchen table and eat. That had been pretty rare though – his mum preferred to make food from scratch. He remembered helping her collect herbs from the garden; she liked the shapes and shades of leaves better than the bright colours of flowers. He always carried the weaved basket that he liked to look through to see the world as a kaleidoscope of colour and she would walk slowly in her long skirt with the big swirls of green, picking fresh-smelling mint and fronds of fennel. They would watch the sun rising beyond the stand of ash trees by the fields, returning over the lawn to the warm kitchen and the smell of bacon cooking, where his dad stood whistling as he listened to classical music on the portable radio that sat on a shelf by the cookery books. Some dark, winter evenings Daniel would sit next to his dad at the piano, learning his chords, his mum on the sofa with its faded woodland motifs, reading a book but listening at the same time and he remembered how, when his dad thought he had learnt enough, he would lean forward himself to play, and Daniel would watch his thin hands flashing over the keys, caressing the music from them, the gold band of his wedding ring catching the light, a comfortable ripple of sound encircling all three of them, the lines and dots of the notes that danced across the pages of the music book seeming to yield the sound themselves, straight from the paper as he followed them. Then he would reach over his dad's arm to turn the page for him, and his dad would smile down at him to say thanks, although he knew the music by heart. Daniel stopped himself. Bill Peters didn't own those moments – why should he be able to invoke them?

He arrived at the apartment block where Sophie lived; 1930s curving brickwork and an art deco frosted glass front door. He pressed the buzzer and the sound of her voice over the intercom brought him back to the present, re-ignited the desire he had felt at the party. He pushed his way through the released door and upstairs to her flat.

"Hi," she stood back to let him in and took his coat.

"Hi. Glad I found the right place."

It was warm, cosy. She led him from the small hallway into a cluttered lounge –

"Sorry for the mess."

"Don't worry." He caught her eye, felt the rush of excitement in the glance.

A candle sent a flickering light across the room from a coffee table littered with academic papers, a potted plant to one side. There was an old sofa, its threadbare covering partly disguised by a green throw, and she sat down, folding her legs underneath her. He sat beside her and they relaxed a bit; she talked about work, the flat, lots of things and he listened. Bringing the moment closer but at the same time holding it back, nervous. She shivered –

"It's cold in here. The heating's rubbish but they won't do anything about it."

"I'll keep you warm."

He put his arm round her and felt her surge towards him, her face close to his, her eyes smiling, their lips touching almost accidentally and then, not playing any more, they kissed and kissed again. Laughing, she pulled away.

"Wait, there's something I want to show you."

She held out her hand and he took it, not speaking, just watching her.

She led him through a door, and they were in her bedroom.

"Look."

There was a big glass tank on a shelf by a bookcase. The light from the tank was the only illumination and peering inside he saw a Praying Mantis balanced on a leaf, its body more like the work of an architect than a living thing, limbs like mechanical parts, blue-green, a rose-pink hue to its abdomen, and its triangle face alien and blank-eyed.

"Do you like her?"

He turned back and put his arms round her again. "She's lovely."

"You know that after sex the female bites off the male's head?"

"I'd heard that, yes." They kissed for a moment. "Should I be worried?"

"Why don't you find out?"

She stared at him, and he pushed her down onto the bed.

Afterwards, while she slept, he got up and dressed. He glanced into the mantid tank and smiled: it was a myth that the males were always eaten by the females – in fact they usually made a quick escape. But the mantid looked up at him with what seemed to him a horrible intent. The green eyes held him. The room jolted around him and suddenly it was a burnt shell, furniture smashed, the door hanging off its hinges. Outside the broken window, trees had sprouted through the tarmac of the street and a wrecked car stood rusting. The mantid raised her arms and brought her pincers together.

Click, Click, Click

The room was itself again. He turned away from the tank and left the flat as fast as he could. Outside he paused and collected himself. Too much cheap Rioja; that and not sleeping enough. The rain had cleared, and a few stars showed beyond the orange of the streetlights, their display brief, the lightening sky to the east dimming their brilliance even as it was revealed. Another day preceded by a breeze that ruffled the water in the puddles and set the trees shivering. Summer was over. He felt suddenly empty.

Kate was not at his flat when he returned, which was no surprise – when he worked late she often slept at her own place, and it was closer to Bill and Susanne's townhouse. Against his usual habit he flicked the radio on in the bedroom and let sleep overtake him as the voices bantered amicably from the ultra-modern speakers, filling the spacious apartment with sound.

Drinking coffee, the next morning in the cafe by the river he sat and tried to focus on his newspaper. He was just relaxing, getting into the flow of the editorial, when someone stepped into his light.

"We need to talk Daniel."

Kate looked more tired and worn even than she had last night. It looked like she hadn't slept.

"Do you want a coffee?" He certainly didn't want this conversation.

"No, I don't want a coffee."

"Well, I've just got a few minutes – I got those papers done but there's still some work to do on my presentation for later."

"Papers? Do you think I'm stupid Daniel?"

He should have guessed –

"You've been talking to Bill Peters, haven't you?"

"He's a friend. I trust him, Daniel."

"He thinks his superstitions put him above everyone else. That he's got some right to meddle in other people's business."

"*We* were friends once, Daniel."

God, she was even using the same phrases as him. Why pretend? – Why not just have it all out in the open? – Everyone played around, it was almost expected –

"You know my philosophy. We're just animals; if we don't follow our instincts, we go crazy."

"Do you believe that, really? – I mean, I know you say it when you're grandstanding to your students – but really?"

What was the point of honesty when people ignored what you

said? "Why should I say something I don't believe?"

"Why should you believe something so fucking stupid?"

"More stupid than God on a cloud? – come on."

"At least they care about other people. We all cared about you. That's why we let you get away with all this – childishness."

"I ..."

"– No. I've had enough of your reasons. You can forget your 'rational' relationship and go and follow your little fawning girls on your own." She slammed something down on the table – the key to his flat. Chubb, brass coloured. And she was gone before he could think of anything to say. The café, hushed momentarily, quickly returned to chatter and feigned to entirely forget the disturbance. He picked up his paper again and carried on reading.

Chapter 5

He would have been able to lean down and cut the boar's throat fairly easily. He'd walked around to the other side of the trap to make the kill, his heart beating hard, knelt down on the loose earth. The flanks of the boar, covered in coarse black hair, had heaved and convulsed as she struggled, and he could still remember the musty hot smell of her. She had been large, a muscular female, in good condition, but all her strength had been impotent to protect her. She'd looked up, and there had been foam at her mouth. Her wet muzzle had quivered. Suddenly her struggling had ceased, and she had become entirely still except for the movement of her breathing. He had looked into her dark eye, edged with fear, and she had met his gaze. Captured by that look, the pulse of adrenalin that made his hands tremble, the rising joy of the kill, had suddenly seemed separate from him, and he recalled feeling as if he was looking in on it. For a second, he'd felt connected to her. He'd sensed her fear – and something more. A solid wall of emotion. Maternal love. And the thought had come to him that he should not kill her. It had come as if implanted in him from outside, not arising from his own mind. It was not right. It was not her time. Slowly he'd lowered the machete and controlled his breathing. Then he'd taken his spade and begun digging the steep front of the pit into a slope that she could climb. Dawn had broken by the time he'd opened up the slope. Then he'd worked loose the stake closest to her head, and her own power had allowed her to dislodge the other. She'd scrambled up the slope, large and magnificent, calling as she moved. And her call had been answered – seven piglets running from the undergrowth where the delicate pale lines on their coats had camouflaged them during their mother's captivity. For a second, she'd looked back, and he'd seen – he imagined he'd seen – recognition in her gaze.

That day he'd left the spade, the salt, the details and the plans behind. Now he kept with him only the basics. Now he knew that nature would provide, that he should only take what was needed for the day.

*

Two days after the break-up, Daniel found himself walking reluctantly up the gravel drive to the Pembertons' sprawling Victorian house. It was almost a mansion in fact – large enough for the columns either side of the front door to feel right, not like the disingenuous flourish of those that adorned the detached houses on the suburban estate near his flat. Of course, the invite had been for Daniel and Kate together – they would never have asked him alone. Pemberton was so fast to the front door that he might have been lurking behind it. He was probably regretting the arrangement too.

"Professor, hello."

Daniel shook the offered hand. "Beautiful house."

"Thank-you Daniel – we like it. I'm just sorry we haven't invited you before, but time passes by so fast."

Now Caroline appeared by his side. "Come on in Daniel."

She led the way along a high-ceilinged hallway with wide stairs ascending into the darkness on one side, and into their front room (or at least, one of them). It was warm and despite its height still managed to be cosy. Light projected gently from a couple of standard lamps, illuminating a wide, soft-looking and slightly battered sofa, an unmatching but obviously comfortable armchair (he guessed from the ragged bunch of articles on the little table at its side that this was Pemberton's corner of the room) a solid oak coffee table with a bunch of spring flowers at its centre, and another less used-looking armchair. A watercolour painting depicting a sweeping upland vista with Turneresque skies hung above the fireplace in which was installed a modern 'real flame' effect fire; there was a bookcase in the corner, heavy laden, and a window seat set into the curved alcove of the bow windows now shrouded by

55

curtains.

"Would you like a drink Daniel? Perhaps a glass of sherry before we eat?"

The drink might soften things a little – "Yes, please."

He sat down on the unevenly lumpy elderly sofa. There was a comfortable feel to the room, but that was overwhelmed by his edginess. Or maybe it was the cause of his edginess? A bit too much like the Peters' place, perhaps? Caroline brought in the drinks and handed them round, Pemberton giving her a warm smile as he reached out from the armchair he had settled into. There was a moment of silence while the professor took courage from his drink.

"Always cheers me up, sherry."

"Yes, it's very good." Daniel's answer stalled the conversation. Caroline tried to revive it –

"Do you remember the dinner party when old Hermanson came around and fell asleep after the first glass? – In the end we had to leave him in here while we had dinner ..."

"Yes, of course – we came back after dessert, and he was snoring."

Daniel raised a smile, and Pemberton laughed. Daniel saw him meet his wife's glance, saw the care in that look. He tried to match it up with the Pemberton of the lecture theatre, the Pemberton who had talked time and again of the evolutionary reasons for the perpetuation of bonds between mates, the rationality of those bonds. Pemberton whose laser-like logic had pared down his own ideas, hammered out the imperfections of thought, dispelled the residual strands of religious belief that he had been unable to completely erase alone.

"What did you do?" He managed to ask naturally while his mind whirred,

"Not much we could do. I think someone (Ted, was it?)."

"Yes, I think it was –"

"Yes, Ted Taylor tried to prod him awake, but he just turned over on his side. Never known anyone like it for sleeping."

"In the end, we just put a blanket over him and left him to it. He got up in the night and went home, and never mentioned it again."

"Probably didn't remember it."

The dinner was tagliatelle in a creamy sauce with cherry tomatoes and salad. Pemberton had made it – his speciality according to Caroline. Small talk and red wine saw Daniel through the pasta and then the homemade chocolate cake with thick cream. As he cleared the last of it, Pemberton sat back in his chair, relaxed by the wine –

"A coffee Daniel? I know I always like one after a meal like that. Cleanse the palette and all that."

"I'll get it Bob."

"No, don't worry darling, you got the drinks before." Pemberton disappeared into the kitchen, and Caroline smiled over at Daniel.

"I know he hasn't invited you over before Daniel, but he does think highly of you. He just likes to keep work separate, that's all."

"Yes, I understand."

"Well, of course, he talks about it a lot, it goes without saying. I can't say I always agree with him but I don't take it too seriously," she lowered her voice conspiratorially. "He's a sentimentalist really – although don't tell him I said that!"

"Don't tell me you said what dear?"

"Nothing, nothing – ah, coffee!"

Daniel watched her pouring. A sentimentalist? Pemberton? The scourge of any theory of human motivation that reached beyond the evolutionary imperative of rational self-interest? It occurred to him, like a hole opening, that the professor did not lead his life by what he taught. While his own stability, his own strategy was founded on

57

those ideas, and beneath it a rock of unquestioning trust. Suddenly these intimate details of Pemberton's life pressed on the sides of that edifice of thoughts like they were an egg, that on its end can support a double decker bus, but just there can be crushed by the gentlest touch. They were talking to him now about the garden and the plants they'd collected over the years. Going to south America to collect seeds for Kew with their baby son. Daniel hadn't even known he'd got a son.

"Hold on, there's a photo here – Caroline leant back and plucked a framed picture off the dresser behind her chair – Alan was about two then."

A younger Pemberton, in his twenties perhaps with a full head of dark tousled hair, wearing a khaki shirt, his son perched in front of him at the wheel of an old jeep, and behind them the extravagant natural entanglement of the jungle.

"Not only did we collect the seeds, but Bob managed to find a new species of beetle."

"Let's not bore poor Daniel with that story. Suffice it to say, I have not always been a dry, shrivelled academic spewing theory from the lectern."

Daniel was silent. Spewing?

"I'm sure he wouldn't be bored – well," she winked at Daniel. "Maybe he would be."

He managed a polite smile.

"But look, I'm forgetting," Pemberton roused himself. "I need to have a chat with you Daniel."

Caroline smiled. "That would be my cue to leave you to it, I think. But," she turned to her husband. "Just one glass of whiskey for you."

A man-to-man whiskey session. He wanted to be on his own. He wanted some time to work things out – but what could he do? He followed the professor through to the front room again.

"Bunnahabhain single malt."

Daniel poised stiffly on the sofa while Pemberton poured, standing at the drinks cabinet with the air of someone who didn't really know where this was going. Now, handing Daniel his glass he moved over to his armchair, perching on its edge.

"So, what do you think about this OPE thing? – I mean, I've got your proposal, but I want to know your personal view."

Daniel looked down at his decanter and tried to marshal the arguments. "I think it could be a game-changer for us – with their resources and our expertise – and Frank and Jill are right behind it, so no problem internally. Even Donald is convinced."

"Yes, good. Good to be on firm ground with this kind of thing. But, erm, I think it will need, well – a bit more thought."

"More thought? Why?"

"Your views." The professor stalled. Daniel's posture became more rigid.

"Our views are the same, aren't they? We need to push back all the cultural superstition and go for the throat. And tapping into the power of OPE, their reach –"

"Daniel," Pemberton drank most of his whiskey in one go and then fiddled with the glass. "I'm afraid our views *aren't* quite the same. Haven't been for a while actually."

Daniel felt that hole opening further. "What?"

"You – well, you apply a very simple logic to everything. Sometimes it doesn't fit."

"But it's what you taught me. How to break things down, to uncover the selective pressures, to find the evolutionary reason."

"Yes, but in a particular context Daniel, in a particular context. You can't just take these evolutionary ideas and apply them to everything. There's more to it than that."

"More to it like what?"

Like love, a tiny voice whispered in Daniel's mind, arising unbidden. *Like love.*

Was this really happening? But – maybe this wasn't from Pemberton at all. He latched onto the idea desperately. "It's the Dean, isn't it? He's started this."

"Who? What? I've been talking to the VC, not ..."

"– First Kate, now you. Those fucking people. Why can't they accept they're wrong?"

Why can't you?

"Daniel, what's this? It's just a funding bid –"

Daniel stood up. "Well, I'll leave you alone. Don't worry. You can act as conscience for someone else."

The Pemberton's lived in one of those select neighbourhoods where wide roads curve gently, lined with trees and ornate streetlamps, where the houses lounge elegantly beyond electronic gates and boundaries of thick shrubs, and pavements roll with the underground thrusts of the roots of proud veteran trees. As Daniel walked away from the house the quietness absorbed his anger, soaked it up in beds of fallen leaves, carried it away into the clouds, invisible above the white orbs of the roadside lights.

He was not much of a drinker, but there was a pub he went to occasionally when he had an article to review or an idea to mull over, and now he needed a drink. It was a crooked, ancient place, sandwiched between shops in the tangle of winding streets in the city centre, like a drunk leaning against more sober friends. Always quiet, an unreformed boozer, walls yellow-brown from years of smoking punters, little corridors and rooms, nooks to slip into and remain undisturbed. The ageing landlord hung onto it like grim death, with nothing else to do with himself – or so Daniel had overheard the regulars say when his back was turned. Daniel never mixed with them – just got his pint and found one of those corners, out of the way.

It was around nine thirty when he got there, ducking in through the low, dark-timbered doorway, to be hit by more noise than usual. But of course, it was Saturday and even here that meant turning up the old juke box, drowning out the silence and the occasional coughing of the old men clearing tar from their lungs. He bought his pint, not quite able to ask for the usual but acknowledged, nonetheless. His appearance may have raised some curiosity from those at the bar used to him coming in early and leaving early, papers under his arm – but if it did, the music drowned it out. He found his way to his usual place, tucked in a little room back from the bar into which only two or three small tables fitted. A heavily shaded lamp in the corner projected a dim light that gave the air a thick, warm quality. He sat, facing an empty wooden chair. To his left on the uneven wall, a black and white photo of the public bar a hundred years ago (the same as now, more or less – did he even recognise some of the patrons?).

So, what now?

From somewhere inside him, the emptiness of the Lord's prayer washed over him again.

Two pints later, and he sat staring down at the table, the beer soaking the minutes away. And then the table was cast into darkness, so that for a moment he thought of the sun sliding behind a cloud, and he looked up. A man had sat down on the chair opposite, between Daniel and the lamp.

"Do you mind if I join you Traveller?"

Daniel's head reeled with the unaccustomed drink – he hadn't accounted for the wine and whiskey at the Pembertons'. He struggled to surface in the warm, dark air. "What? Did you say –?"

"It's not important. I'm just resting my legs."

Daniel could only make out the silhouette of a broad head and thick beard, a heavy coat that the man did not remove. Daniel smelt

61

– something. He tried to place it – wood? soil? vegetation? A mix of those. Perhaps, the smell you get in a forest after rain. There was a long pause – not a silence, the jukebox didn't permit that – and Daniel drank some more. He wasn't usually bothered by people in this way. The locals were old enough to remember deference, its invisible layers like the layers of residue on the walls. He could feel the man watching him.

"I wonder, why are you sitting here on your own?"

"I'm minding my own business."

"It's funny, isn't it, how people share ideas they don't believe in."

"How –?"

"They don't do it on purpose, you know. Well, most of them don't. It's just, they have other things to think about. They just learn as much as they need to say something that people think has a value."

"Yes. Hypocrisy."

"Humanity. I wasn't blaming them – everyone has limits. Except you maybe? I mean, that's what you think, isn't it?"

"Like I said, I'm minding my own business. Find someone else to bother."

"Well, I'm being unfair. You know you have limits – who can avoid learning that? But you can see further."

"Well, that's what I keep being paid for, so I would hope so."

"Everyone would hope so. But it's not really seeing further is it – taking some idea and applying it to everything?"

Not this again.

"You're saying I'm an idiot." Daniel stared at the man, towards his face in general, not being able to make out his eyes. If only he could focus properly. "I'm an idiot to follow the logic of an idea?"

"No, you're not an idiot. You just have a need to rely on

something."

"Do I really?"

"But even logic is limited. If you can reduce people to being self-interest machines, that doesn't necessarily mean that that's all they are. Parsimony is an assumption."

Now he saw what this conversation was. "Nice line. What are you on?"

Bar room philosophers, the town was crammed with them. All you had to do was engage and out poured the clever turns of phrase and the deep meanings as fast as beer from the pumps – except it took no effort to bring it to the glass, only to stop it. "Go on then, lay on the crap. What is it this time – yogic thought waves?"

"You are certain of science, certainly. You were just as certain about religion though, weren't you?"

Or at least, it sounded as though that's what he said – a crashing heavy metal track had exploded from the jukebox as he spoke. But he couldn't have said that. "What? I can't hear you. Leave me alone for fucks sake."

"You keep letting yourself be brimmed full by them, one after another, don't you? – other people's ideas. What are *you*? Who are *you*?"

For some reason he could not understand, his mind suddenly went back to a camping trip he'd once been on with scouts. They'd built bivouacs from fallen branches and bracken and turf, learned what berries and roots they could eat – then had instant noodles. Rain-laced woods echoing with bird calls, the drift of smoke from the campfire.

"There is something then, something to you."

"Why –? What are you –? "

"If you're not strong enough, those things get buried."

He remembered trying to outdo his friends in fire-lighting. That was the thing that had always impressed people most. The elemental power of it.

"Nature has no ideas to force on you. Only experiences."

Those memories linked to other memories, and those to yet others, and led him where he would rather not go.

"NO."

"But still, you have to go there."

"Into the past? For what?"

"Not into the past. Into nature again."

And suddenly he imagined swimming out to sea from a pebble beach. He could just carry on, out and away if he wanted. The next thing he knew, he felt a tentative touch on his shoulder.

"Come on sir, home time. Not like you to get in a state."

"What?" Daniel stared around him, working out where he was. "Oh – yes – of course." He gazed in confusion at the empty chair opposite.

The landlord looked tired. "Like I said sir, home time. Come on, on with your coat"

Dazed, Daniel struggled into his jacket and made his way uncertainly out of the room and across the bar to the door, struggled with the latch, got out into the cool night air.

He didn't wake up until noon and when he did it was with a splitting headache. Over a large coffee and bread and marmalade (it would have been toast, but Kate had taken the toaster away and he couldn't face fiddling with the grill) he tried to piece together the night before. Who the hell had that weirdo in the bar been? But then, the landlord had had to kick him out – had he dreamt him? God, he'd been asleep on the table. He remembered seeing the pint glass sideways on. The tabletop had been sticky with spilt lager. He nearly retched. That explained the smell of stale beer. Doubtless the publican would be telling the old guys at the bar about how he'd ended up. He could forget their deferential respect. Then, with a lurch, he remembered why he had been there. Pemberton's shocked face swam up through the haze and he put his coffee down and lay back on the sofa, feeling the room spin. He took some deep breaths and, as things steadied, he tried to remember what that bearded man had been going on about. Something about going back to nature. It was Sunday he realised – if he wanted to eat later, he would have to get down to the supermarket before four. Kate used to do that, if he was busy. No need yet though. Maybe a DVD – something gentle. But his eyes slid over empty shelves – not his. What had been his?

"Who are you?"

Beyond those reference books and articles stacked on the floor by the coffee table?

"Brimmed full by them."

He made it over to the kitchen cupboard and found the paracetamols. Swallowing a couple with a glass of water he stood for a while and looked out of the front window – he had thought standing up for a bit might help, but it didn't. Over the road was a little park; a few horse chestnut trees stood there, heavy with browning leaves. He thought of woods and meandering streams. He had known something, that man. Not like most of that type. What he'd said about nature – there was something in that. The simplicity of it – surviving, not putting on any front. He looked around the flat, spotted a space where there had been a picture on the wall, looked back outside. Perhaps he could find some peace out there, away from everyone. He sat back on the sofa again and massaged his head with his fingertips. Maybe – it wasn't a long-term solution, he realised that – but maybe for a while he could get out there, into the hills. Thinking about it, he knew a few places – could just about remember them anyway. Just a temporary respite – a few weeks. Maybe a couple of months at most. A sabbatical – he could sell that idea to the university, he was sure of it. Worry about everything else when he got back.

Chapter 6

Daniel felt the shop assistant watching him as he collected what he needed. He hadn't shaved for days. He explored the shelves, focussing on the basics: a knife and sharpening stone, a machete, a light fold-away spade, a simple first aid kit, an ultra-light tent. He already had salt for preserving meat and antiseptic for cleaning wounds, waterproof sealable packets for storing gathered food. Outside, the streets were busy – workers turning out of offices for an early lunch, newspapers on sale at the stand on the corner. Raindrops spread circles across the puddles as he walked back to his motorbike – his early mid-life crisis, Kate called it – his survival gear already packed in his rucksack. A lady passed, hunched beneath an umbrella, a bag of shopping in her hand, a 'Weetabix' box at the top, a tin of Heinz soup pressed against the plastic. An ache of sadness passed over him. Once on the bike, he rode fast, the force of the engine taking him beyond the familiar – beyond the arms of the city, the soft agricultural padding that held it, beyond motorway and trunk road, beyond tarmac – up into the northern mountains.

He left the bike at a garage in a hamlet at the head of a wide glacial valley, paying the owner for the storage. The corrugated iron mechanics' shed seemed caught in an earlier decade: rusting unsheltered pumps, a tiny office with faded posters of racing cars and topless women, an ageing attendant. Except for the man, the huddle of houses appeared deserted. He walked for two hours, following a stream to its source, a sodden bed of rushes on a high plateau. Crossing this, he set up his tent with the last of the daylight, amid the first trees of a woodland that stretched away into the night. By torchlight he collected enough wood for a fire and cooked a packet rice. The tent, water, packet food, torch, were stop-gaps until he found a permanent place to stay, built his own shelter, began to forage.

It was a clear night and the stars were myriad, the bright familiar constellations joined by countless others, the Milky Way like a sprinkled trail of fine white powder. He slept deeply, and at dawn woke and ate a couple of cereal bars before striking camp, heading downhill into open, deer-tended forest. Birdsong echoed, its backdrop a silence only softened by the sough of a light breeze that shook the canopy of the trees. He took in every detail of the landscape, every movement: the dark moss-covered tree roots, a red squirrel chasing lightly along the branches of a Scots Pine, open stretches of heather and bilberry, the twisting, glittering courses of mountain streams. Attuning his eyes to opportunity and risk, turning his thoughts to the practical. By the end of the second day, he felt he had travelled far enough. It was as if he was in a completely new world. Slowing his pace, he started to look for a suitable place to make a more permanent camp. After a while, he found some dry ground close to a stream. There was an open space between the trees just wide enough to let the heat of the sun through in the middle of the day. Shelter, water, warmth.

The next morning, he began to make a bivouac; cutting saplings to make a flexible frame, building up layers of branches and turf, just as he had as a teenager, playing at survival in that softer landscape around his parents' home. He let himself be absorbed completely in his work. His first days on those forested slopes were an adventure. He had a sense of childlike excitement, remembering the rules of survival that had lain unused in his mind for years, revelling in his freedom from the constraints of the norms of modern existence. The early autumn woods and hills were ready to be harvested. The tasks of foraging and hunting brought satisfaction with their mastering, and his efforts brought reward; hazelnuts, acorns and sweet chestnuts collected in bags and hidden in hollow trees or the cool recesses of fissures in the rocks.

He had not brought a watch with him, consciously trying to attune himself to natural cycles and rhythms. The days and nights passed, and he began to understand more about his body – he tried not just to feel physical desires like hunger but to explore them more deeply, to hone his perception of them; which plants his body needed, which meat. He worked alongside squirrels and jays, the flocks of tits that fed in the birch trees. He ate blackberries and cherries, learnt to stomach and even to enjoy the bitter green crab apples, found bilberries and crowberries on the moors. Like the badger he dug for roots; the tubers of silverweed like mean, thin potatoes, the delicate bulb of the pignut, seeds of the balsam that grew by fast running streams, the refreshing foliage of golden saxifrage. To work with those wild creatures, to labour with them as an equal, to engage in the mechanics of survival with the same full and necessary commitment, he felt not as a burden but as a release. He remembered the lessons he had learned on his childhood camping trips, he learned new ones. Even his mother's knowledge came back to him, despite his resolution to avoid those family memories. His shelter he reinforced with heavy turfs as insulation, and he had a fire at its entrance. Close by he dug out an earth oven for slow cooking meat and hanging from the trees he had arranged a tarpaulin to catch rainwater and dew.

His accomplishments and progress buoyed him, and he slept deeply and worked hard. The other world retreated in his mind until he almost believed that it had given up its hold. Physical labour focussed his thoughts in the present, and past and future were in abeyance. Nature's challenges were part of a system, and experience allowed him to read the signs that that system gave of coming change. People brought the extremes, the unexpected. His new life was freedom; a solitary fight against the opponent of nature. His temporary solution came to seem permanent, and he found that he did not want to return to a life that now seemed like the existence of a prisoner. He had pushed beyond the outer markers, left the garden, broken its bounds.

Inefficiently at first, he trapped rabbits and caught fish. As autumn hardened to winter, he relied more on these successes and felt his failures more keenly. Berries and nuts had been cleaned from the trees and foliage decayed. His stores began to dwindle and the animals he hunted seemed harder, wilier and less wholesome when consumed. Darkness ate away at the morning and the evening and his ability to forage was diminished with the light. It became colder and the rain became persistent. He had chosen a well-drained site for his camp and his clothes were high quality, but dampness still pervaded until it seemed it was a part of him, within as well as without; it crept in as the fire shrank at the end of each evening and receded with sullen reluctance when he coaxed the flames back in the thin mornings as drizzle drifted down between the trees. When there was no rain there was frost, and he would wake to find his campsite glittering as if it was sugar-coated and he had to force himself from the protective shell of his survival bag into the frozen air and heat smashed ice in his mess tin to drink. He could not wash, and the only benefit of the cold was that there were no fleas or tics to torment him.

He had taken with him a wind-up radio, to keep in touch with the news from the world he had left behind. Through September and October, it remained wrapped in plastic and he did not even think of it; the novelty of his new life did not leave him the time to consider the outside world. To rebuild a connection to it could only bring back unwanted memories. But as the weather grew bitter and the nights drew in, the desire for that connection with the rest of humanity grew. His initial euphoria subsided, and he found that the struggle to collect food, to sleep and live in this wilderness, became a focus for his negativity rather than a tonic for it.

At last he gave in, found the radio in its plastic packing tucked into a recess at the back of the bivouac. Ashamed of his capitulation, like an alcoholic ordering a pint, he unpacked the moulded plastic box, unhooked the handle at the back and, with regular turns, powered the dynamo. The mechanical whir sounded strange after months without artificial noise, disturbing in the sudden divide it created between him and nature. And the voices that followed were more of a shock, cheerfully reverberating around the clearing. He turned the volume down low, finding that the sound unsettled him more than the darkness of the winter. Switching it off, he wrapped the radio away and put it back out of sight. At the same time, he realised that he would have to keep that connection. Not only did he need to stay up to date with what was happening outside, he also needed to keep hold of his ability to communicate, to fit back in. However appealing, this wild life was a fantasy that could only be lived out for so long.

The winter dragged on and closed in, and although it was not the hardest or the coldest he had known, it was more than enough to test him. By mid-January, snow lay on iron hard ground. His autumn fat had burnt from him so that he was gaunt and bright-eyed with eagerness to grasp any opportunity of food. The radio bought news of unsettling developments back in that other world of technology and people. In the space of a few days, unsettling became horrifying. In an apparently random geographical pattern, large numbers of people had started to go down with a strain of influenza not seen before. It was being treated as bioterrorism – the spread was wrong for a natural outbreak, the strain too different from those in existence before. A secure lab broken into somewhere? The virus released in places that would maximise infection rates? No-one admitted to doing it.

The reports suggested the virus had a long, contagious incubation period – around ten days. And the new strain had only been isolated four days after the symptoms had developed in the first patients. Thousands were already infected at that point. The virus was virulent. It didn't respond to treatment and Daniel knew it would be mutating as it spread. The survival rate after five days of infection was estimated at around two percent. He did the maths. He reckoned mortality could be seventy percent. Could that be right?

As the days passed, live broadcasts were replaced by recorded ones, repeated by unfamiliar presenters. Fewer reports all the time, looping round. Pleas, to ignore social media and the conspiracy theories: blaming minority groups or the government, claiming that the virus wasn't real, that it was in the water supply or had been administered through aeroplane chem trails. Those pleas had soon changed to pleas to refrain from violence, not to ignore advice, not to attack medical centres. As he listened, he saw in his mind the green eyes of the mantid. It was too big to take in. Or was he so

70

isolated that he'd lost his empathy? His lack of reaction took him further from it, as if he was an observer from another planet, charting in reverse man's rise to civilisation. In the end that's what made him retrace his journey through the miles of woodland, over the mountain pass. He needed to see it, to feel it, to know if it was real.

The majestic ice-carved valley stretched away from him, a stream twisting at its heart, the now unfamiliar geometric patterns of walls and hedges laid out around it. There was the hamlet, the cluster of houses, the garage. From here it seemed so peaceful and ordinary that he started to doubt what he'd been hearing. Had he been alone so long he'd started to hallucinate? He'd heard once about a cave far up in the scorched hills of north Africa where people went to find themselves, how in the silence and solitude they had disturbing visions, strange experiences. Still, he approached the village over the fields, not by the track that turned into a metal road at the edge of the houses. The buildings seemed as silent and empty as they had that day when he'd arrived. There was the old garage. That looked the same too, but it didn't feel the same and he watched it for a long time before he went closer. He was the only thing that was moving. Maybe the garage was just shut down – it was hardly bustling before. In the garden closest to it weeds grew tall and rank. The front door of the house was ajar. The day was so still that even the old, battered engine oil sign hung still in its corroding frame. Weeds had sprung up at the joins in the concrete apron. The glass door was closed, but its glass was smashed in. Maybe the place had been evacuated. Like Chernobyl.

Find out what you want fast and get out.

He took a deep breath and broke cover by the garden hedges, jogging across the open space, past the derelict pumps, stepping through the empty doorframe without pausing, as if positivity would drive back any danger. The shelves by the counter had been cleared. He had been hoping to find a newspaper but there were none. There were papers on the floor though – flyers. He picked one up carefully from amongst the broken glass from the door and read it. The simple, innocuous title was in bold, red type:

"HM Government, Ministry of Health: General instruction 17"

The rest was not so innocuous.

"The orders below are mandatory and necessary for your safety and that of others. Transgressors will be fined max £2000 and risk remote physical enforcement action."

(What did that clumsy euphemism stand for, he wondered?).

"All residents: Remain in your homes to avoid contact with / spread of the influenza virus. Food will be delivered at regular intervals. Do not approach the operatives. Keep your distance from others collecting rations. One pack only per person per delivery. The packs include disinfectant gels and sprays. Spray sterilise outer packaging before use. No travel is permitted beyond one mile from your residence."

"Multi-person households: Sleep in separate rooms and prepare food separately. Disinfect all shared utilities after use. Anyone feeling unwell should be isolated and medical services should be informed using the number below."

"Single person households: Do not approach neighbours or friends. Maintain contact via social media and telephone only. In case of illness, inform the authorities using the number below. Inform all those you have had recent contact with. Collect your food pack from the separate pile on delivery (red packs)."

It hadn't been a hallucination. The message was dated January 15th. It must be early February by now.

It didn't say leave.

He spun round, but the forecourt outside was as empty and still as before. The houses were blank-faced. He knew what it might mean to meet someone who was sick. Something struck him then about his life in the woods – all that attention to detail and yet he'd never once thought about illness – not this, but just getting sick. He'd packed some painkillers but for some reason he'd never thought beyond that. Arrogance? Maybe, but on the other hand, he hadn't got ill. His immune system might have strengthened with exposure to the environment. While sterilising everything – it was like hiding in a shrinking space.

Get out now.

One more thing though. Having his bike would be useful (it had still had half a tank of fuel left in it, if he remembered right). He could wheel it up to one of the little barns out of the village. Insurance if he needed it, although he wasn't sure where he might want to go. He stepped out through the doorway again, and moved slowly round to the workshop, not gung-ho anymore. The big, corrugated iron doors stood open. In the gloom inside a topless girl still cast down a sultry stare from the calendar over the desk in the little office. He found his keys in there, hung up at the back where he remembered the old man putting them. He'd wheeled his bike to the back, but it was hard to see if it was still there – there were no windows and he wasn't about to try the lights. He edged around a car parked over the inspection pit – its bonnet was up and bits of its engine were laid out on a bench against the wall. His heart sank – no bike, nothing but scattered spare parts and old oil drums and boxes and tyres. Suddenly the shadows changed.

"Please, can you help me?"

No, no, no.

By the car he had just worked his way around was a young boy. He was clutching onto the vehicle, pale and sweating.

"I'm sorry."

"Please."

The boy moved towards him around the car, looking at him.

The other side – get around.

73

He was faster and healthy. It wasn't hard to get out. He ran back across the apron, up the track. As he reached the saddle at the top of the valley he looked back over that sweeping view, the village that looked as peaceful as before, the fields, the road back towards the city. He realised he would have to give up his encampment. Two day's walk wasn't far enough away. If there were more survivors surely at least some of them would head for the uplands? Unless they were all too afraid after Instruction 17. He didn't think of going back. Not to that.

The next morning, he pulled apart his shelter, scattering its parts in the woods he had come to know so well. He gathered as much of his stored food as he could, folded the tarpaulin down into a bundle tight enough to fit on top of his pack, and left, denying himself even a backward glance. He walked deeper into the hills, higher up where the trees were less dense.

In time, with the advancing spring, came a sense of freedom, a fading of the memory of the garage and the boy. Now when he checked the radio, he found only static. Was that it? Despite the flyer he had expected lines of refugees, troops, encampments. They didn't come. Once he came across a tent in a clearing, but the fear that ran through him was unmerited. The young couple, lying amid the new life of spring, were dead, their bodies stirring with maggots.

A belief grew in him that the vision of the mantid had been a warning. Some jump, from zealous reductionism to belief in the psychic powers of an insect. But, underneath, he argued to himself, it was all the same. Hard-wired instinct triggering emotions, making the connections that assured the safest choices. Even the mystical could be disassembled, its roots traced, its magic revealed as mechanics. His real worry now, was illness – any illness, not just the flu. Things were no different for him than before, but now he knew he had no safety net. His fantasy was reality, and the reality he had escaped from had become the fantasy. But the routines of survival remained constant, required immediate attention; helped him ignore what lay beyond. In time, he started to doubt himself again. Perhaps even that trip to the village had been in his mind. Perhaps he had never had a radio? Perhaps it was all still there, if he just walked a few days south? Or perhaps it had never been there. He flung himself into nature. Not playing any more, just surviving, like any other animal.

∗

Freshness – rain, but not yet. Hunger. He pawed the ground for the tubers. Whiteness in the brown. A bitter taste, fleshy. Moving between patches he loped on feet and hands. Another hunger. Look up, away from the ground. Green, prickles, red. He took the raspberries one by one, eagerly. The rain came, lightly. Feeling it on his skin he bounded back to the hollow in the tree. Warm closeness of wood. He picked woodlice off the bark and ate them, staring out into the downpour. He slept, darkness enveloped him and the tree. Sadness. Woman. The sun rose. Warmth, the scent of drying soil. Hunger. He followed the earth-vegetable smell to another patch of tubers, nose low. Dragged at the earth and the plants. Whiteness. Fleshy bitterness. Another hunger. In the soil, pink flesh. He pulled and took it to his mouth. Pull and chew, pull and chew. Stop. Danger. Hot mustiness, heaviness. He turned and raised himself up.

"Aaagggghhh."

The boar turned away. He settled again, fingers finding the grass. Cool. Safety. Hunger. Hands in the earth.

Seasons turned. Years turned. And still he was not part of it. Still he imagined the old world in his dreams. Still he could not see what was in front of him without seeing what there could be and what their might have been. And then. A dew-drenched spring dawn. He opened his eyes, disturbed. Saw feeble light on the tree trunks. What had woken him? Magpies quarrelled on bare branches. Not that, not them. Something else, close. He turned his head a fraction and saw. A man. Close by him. Hands in the hollow beside him. Fumbling with his old bag. Anger. Fear. Silence, a heave of wheezing breath. Adrenalin. Daniel's hand was around the club, by him in the dark.

The man ignored him. Daniel raised himself and the club. Smashed it down across the man's shoulders. The man crumpled, emaciated, hardly struggling. Weakness. Rage. Hatred. Club gripped tight and brought down again across the weather-beaten face. Release. Swish and thud, swish and thud. And the man was lifeless. The scent changed. Death. Emptiness. He stared down at a caved in skull in the grey morning light.

Lurching out of the hollow he grabbed his bag and stumbled away. He turned once to see a magpie spiral down to pick a brass button from the man's coat. It flew up again with a laugh as the first crow began its descent from the cloud-streaked sky. He retched, loped away. But he was awake again inside. He stretched up, felt the sinews pull, unaccustomed to it, and ran on his legs alone. He fell, he ran again. The air was cold now, the trees around him dark and crooked, the ground rough. He had killed a man. The chattering of feeding birds jarred, a dumb clamour.

There was nobody around. Nature continued. He did not forage. He was separate. He wandered through the day, stopping only when there was so little light that he found himself falling against the roots that snaked across the black earth. He sat down with his back against a tree, senseless to the cold. Half sleeping, he saw only his wooden club descending, again and again.

"And the LORD God said, Behold, the man is become as one of us, to know good and evil."

Snow began to fall. His face was hot. Somehow, he forced himself to stand. The snowfall thickened to a blizzard as he struggled downhill beside a frozen stream. In front of him between the shards of snow, he saw a cottage, crouched low between the stream and the trees. A warm glow sprang out from the house across the whiteness. A lighted window in a storm. Something to be evaded, something dangerous. But he was desperate. With a mixture of fear and longing he circled the building, reverting to all-fours again, moving closer with the suspicious tread of a wolf approaching a prey that is still alive, still has teeth. He could see little, was forced by dizziness and fatigue to the porch. He knocked, bounded back and tried to tense himself, only to fall sideways against a low wall as the door opened. Light streamed across his prone, semi-conscious form. The silhouette of a man with a pistol was framed in the glow.

Chapter 7

When he woke, he had a feeling of being somewhere, sometime else. He lay under warm, clean sheets on a soft mattress and heard music – Vaughan Williams' 'Lark Ascending' – drifting from another room. He smelt frying eggs and saw the morning sun pouring through a small window to fill the room. He felt, then, that he was home, in Surrey; he could sense the rolling hills, the streams waiting for his exploration, the welcome from his parents as he arrived back exhausted, the big, blackened kettle beginning to whistle on the hob. But the veil of his imagination was stretched too thinly. He saw his battered, patched bag on a chair and, looking more closely at the window, realised that it was not bolted nor locked but nailed shut. He dragged the bed clothes to the floor and on all fours pulled himself to the corner of the room and curled up there. He was breathing heavily, wheezing.

Shortly afterwards he heard a key turn in the door lock but he was too weak to react. An old man entered cautiously, his gun held inexpertly but steadily in his right hand, and in odd contrast a mug of tea in the other. Daniel tried to speak. But he could produce only a guttural growl. The man looked at him.

"Get up. Get off the floor. You're not an animal."

Under the muzzle of the gun, Daniel crawled to the bed, onto it, pulling the bedclothes around him again.

"Right. Drink this like a human being."

Daniel drank, holding the mug in both hands, guzzling the hot tea. He tried to speak again, and again there was only an incoherent, rasping cry. The old man closed the door.

"I am a fool or a madman," he said as, treading with a limp, he moved on slightly bowed legs to the side of the bed. The gun remained steadily aimed. He was a short man, bald with wisps of white hair stretching around the back of his head from one ear to the other, the bare patch mottled with liver spots. His face was deeply lined, bearded, tanned.

"I show a light, I answer the door, and I let death in, by murder or disease."

He moved Daniel's knapsack and clothing to the floor and sat without taking his eyes off his patient.

"I am Carl, and today I am a lucky fool because you are too weak to kill, and your ailments are exposure and a chest infection, and not the flu."

He smiled, his teeth almost as white as his beard and hair. His eyes were walnut brown, with a shadow behind them. Maybe fear, maybe sadness. Maybe both.

"And you too," he jabbed his finger. "You're a lucky fool, because I'm not a killer, and I've been away from anyone and anything for long enough to know I'm not contagious. Doubly lucky, because I'm a doctor, although I'm afraid I've got no medicine."

He lent back and lifted up the remnants of a wallet that Daniel still carried in his bag for him to see. Daniel had ceased using anything in that bag a long time ago. But he needed it. He had killed for it.

"You are Daniel – unless this is stolen. And it would be futile to carry around a stolen wallet – although," he added, "no more futile than anything else."

Daniel propped himself up. This man, Carl, was right. He was a fool for coming here, and he was scared. Not just of Carl. It was the low ceiling of the room, the clutter of furniture, the heavy windows. The doctor must have read the look in his eyes.

"Listen," he said, leaning forward and lowering the gun for the first time. "We're both scared. We've both been scarred by what we've seen, by what we imagine. So, we can't trust each other. Or ourselves," he added, watching Daniel closely.

"But here we are. You can't survive outside, or without my help; you have no choice but to accept my charity. I'm in control. But after a time, if you recover, the tables turn – you become a threat to me."

Daniel glanced at the gun.

"No – even with this an old man like me is not safe – I have to sleep, and I'm slow. Who knows what you might do to get supplies from me, or just in the throes of some delusional episode? So, this is what will happen. This door," he pointed to the door he had entered by. "I will leave open – wide open."

Daniel nodded. He had forgotten the care that one person could show to another.

"The outside door is bolted, always," Carl went on. "But it can be opened from inside. It's on the right. So, you can always leave. The other doors – to my rooms – will be locked all the time."

He stood up and shuffled towards the door.

"I'll bring you food and drink from my supplies. And some clothes."

He left the door open behind him, and Daniel heard the jangle of keys as he unlocked his own quarters and disappeared within. Then he settled back on the pillows to sleep. He dreamt of the white roots and the red berries, worms and frost, leaves and boar, the hollow in the tree, a smashed skull.

He woke, it was night. He felt his awareness of thought and of future and past stretching out from him again, beyond present, beyond sense. He felt with his mind the before. He saw the boy in the garage and his encampment, he saw Pemberton and he saw Kate. Was that all him? What stood between him and that? The room was pitch dark – the black-out curtains that stopped any light escaping stopped any getting in too. He delved into the last four years, half afraid of what he might find. There were only fragments, like remembering the gaps in a drunken night out. Four years – he remembered that much – four times four seasons had passed, measured somewhere in his sub-conscious. He slept again.

Over the next few days, Carl talked to him and, each day, coaxed first words, and then sentences from him. Forced his brain to follow the old pathways again. Reeled him in from the edge of the divide. Patterns reasserted themselves. He embraced them, distanced himself from what came before, tried to sew up the wound, bringing the skin of now and before together over that gap. Short exchanges, little insights moved him forward – how Carl had been a doctor before the End, his enjoyment of fine art that was now out of reach. A few words about Daniel's academic life, shared more guardedly but shared, nonetheless.

Daniel learnt Carl's routine. Each morning the old man would take his field glasses and climb the western ridge overlooking the cottage, from which vantage point he could see perhaps ten miles down the valley and spot a plume of smoke much further away. He made the excursion partly from sentimentality, he said – he had buried his dog, a big, quiet Pointer, up on the hill. To keep watch. He even marked the spot with a wooden cross, positioned off the skyline so as not to leave a sign of his presence. At lunchtime and in the evening, he would bring Daniel food; there was a basement beneath the cottage, and that was the source of the old man's supplies – fresh things he foraged for, except for the eggs which he took from the ducks he had penned at the back of the cottage.

The routine was a comfort to Daniel; it enveloped him in a sense of humanity he had drifted from, built a wall against the memory of the swirl of events that had claimed him. Ten days passed and there was trust and affection between the two men. But Daniel's condition had worsened. In the evening of the Monday after his arrival – Carl had hand-written calendars to keep track of the days and the dates – Daniel's chest hurt so much that it was painful to breath. When Carl brought him soup, he saw he was struggling.

"I'll get you some painkillers – I've got strong ones, all that's left of my old supplies I'm afraid."

"What if I had had the flu?"

"Then I'd be dead. But I'm not."

Was that disappointment? He left the room, returning a minute later with two light blue tablets and a glass of water. Daniel swallowed them down. His wheezing was loud in the silence, and he spoke to hide it – or perhaps I need to get something off my chest, he thought sardonically. But it wasn't funny, any of it.

"I never asked – where were you a doctor?"

"A little village in Cumbria – edge of the lakes. One of those places where everyone knows everyone else."

He turned away, as if to go, but Daniel wanted to take his mind off his own breathing, and his own thoughts.

"Did you like it?"

The old man turned back slowly to his patient.

"I loved the job, I loved the place." He sat down and stared out of the nailed-down window at the ridge that shouldered out the tangerine-sunset sky. "That is, I liked it at first. For years I liked it. Then my wife died."

"I'm sorry ..."

"Don't worry. A fair few others have died since then. That was before it all started. Cancer. Quick really. After that the place was just too full of memories – but I only had two years to go to retirement, so I had to stay, to finish the job."

"Finish the job?"

"I'd cared for those people for years; I didn't want to leave them until I stopped working. I wanted to help them for as long as I could," he laughed. "Commendable? – yes, I can see it in your face. Except of course that I didn't."

"What do you – ?"

"Never mind, never mind," he waved the question away and changed tone. "What about you? Where was your university?"

Daniel told him, then struggled to think what else to say. For these last days, he had been torn between the desire to talk, and a reluctance to tell Carl about what he had been before, how he had lived, how naïve he had been.

"You never mentioned any family." Of course, it was natural for him to wonder.

"No, I was single. My parents died when I was quite young – while I was at uni."

"Then we both have losses to grieve for. Not just the ones at the End. Funny how the ones before seem more real isn't it?"

"I don't know, I didn't see it – the End I mean."

He didn't mention that other encounter, that other death.

"No?"

"I left," Daniel wheezed and coughed and regained his voice. "I ran away, like a kid. I was a kid, I guess. I wanted to be on my own. That was before the End. I heard about it on an old radio – I just saw one little boy in a village. He wanted my help. But I ran away from him too." Another fit of coughing racked him.

"Do you want some more painkillers?"

"No, no." He held out his hand to stop the old man leaving. He wanted to know what he'd seen.

"Please, tell me. What was it like?"

Carl sighed. He stood up and drew the curtains across the window, expelling the dying rays of sunshine. Now the room was illuminated entirely by the gas lamp he had brought in at dusk. He sat back down –

"I suppose I've had nobody to tell, and I'm unlikely to find anyone else. So, I might as well tell you." He sat quietly for a while before he started to speak. "At first, it was like any other crisis – it seemed distant – especially from the village. The idea of new flu strains wasn't new; bird flu and swine flu and all that. I'd been reading about them for years. But this was different. Bio-terrorism they said. Who knows the truth of it? – the lies multiplied so fast. I remember it was the suddenness of the whole things that was most shocking. They started saying there was a new flu virus, a day later that it was deadly, and two days later the first cases were reported in the village. They were isolated of course – I had to go out to them in biohazard gear delivered from some government depot. That made it worse for the children." He paused for a moment. "People I had known for years were dying, and I couldn't do anything. Can you imagine that, in the 21st century, in England for God's sake? Suddenly we weren't safe, we weren't modern and civilised – we were out in nature. Everyone knew there was nothing I could do, but of course sometimes they would blame me – say I should have acted faster or done something different. Who else could they blame?"

The old man turned the knob on the gas light, and it roared louder, and the light brightened. Holding back the dark. "The whole system was starting to collapse. That's when you realise how flimsy things are. Everything built on trust, everyone relying on 'them' to sort things out. Until they realise there is no 'them', just other people. And that barrage of conspiracy theories on social media – anything the government tried to do, there'd be a dozen alternative treatments that went against their advice, even theories that the instructions were just a plan spread the virus faster. People didn't know what to believe."

"What did you do? Just carry on?"

"Ha ha. Well, that was the plan. My noble ambition. But in the end, I fucked off and left them." The rushing breath of the lamp was loud behind his voice. "I fucked off and left them."

There was silence. Daniel almost spoke, but now the doctor continued his story matter-of-factly; he was safely back amid the practical details.

"Getting the opportunity was so lucky that I was able to think of it as fate, something out of my hands. A man died, out at the edge of the village; I went out to check on him and found the body. I'd known him a long time – I knew he had no family. I knew that he'd spent most of the money he earned on a house up in the hills – this place." He waved his arm round the room, flickering in and out of reality with the guttering light.

"For some reason, he never moved into it. I think when it came down to it the idea of isolation was better as a dream than a reality. But from all my visits I knew exactly where he kept all his keys. By that time the idea of legal processes had long since slipped; just disposing of a body hygienically was hard enough. Even with martial law and all their 'Instructions'. So, I reported the death, for what good it would do – took the keys and left the same day."

Behind his eyes moved images of people who had been alive when he left, people who must surely have perished in the weeks that followed, their faces the fabric of the shadow that darkened his eyes. Again, silence fell, and Daniel filled it, although his words echoed hollowly in the vaulted emptiness of the old man's guilt, came back to him as a retort:

"You stayed as long as you could."

"They had no-one."

"You couldn't help them anyway."

"But I could have been there for them."

Daniel stopped, looked down at his battered hands.

"At least you stayed until it got too bad. I left before it started."

"Then you couldn't have known ..."

"It's not just that ..."

But he could not admit what else it was that troubled him, even now, even in this confessional space. The lamp hissed, the time passed. In another world, a clock would have ticked, but time was not measured now, except by the ebb and flow of life, the changing seasons, their persistent variation that could not be ignored.

However hard one tried. Carl did not ask what it was he had wanted to say. Maybe he was too lost in his own past, or maybe he didn't want to know.

Carl disappeared back to his rooms, brought back a dusty bottle of whisky and a jug of water, poured liberally and passed a glass to Daniel. It burnt his throat, but he still drank it. Not as smooth as the Bunnahabhain single malt all those years ago. Before all this. Eventually, the old man broke the silence, launched into his own reverie, and the moment, the chance for Daniel to share, passed and was lost in the flow of his voice and the flow of whisky.

"In a way the virus wasn't the worst of it. The reactions were harder – people's minds twisted by fear. All that blame and hatred. The parliamentary massacre."

But he veered away from that. Driven by the fire of the drink, his mind seemed to be on causes, the wide sweep of things, the black and white beyond the doubt and shame of personal greys.

"Diseases don't wipe out civilisations on their own – it was that hatred and fear that did it. You know how it was, before – the divisions, the blame, the rich getting richer and the poor getting poorer. The cracks opening little by little."

Pouring another whisky Carl got carried away with his anger and with the drink. He was righteous, Daniel wheezing, darkened with the knowledge of his own hatred, the injustice he had meted out with all the ferocity that Carl was describing. The old man thought he was with another good man, with a soulmate, and it seemed there was no space any more to tell him what he needed to.

"The gospel of the market," Carl's hands raised in imitation of a preacher. "The creed of flexibility, the Lord's prayer of competition spread with evangelical zeal."

The lamp flickered in a cold breeze that swept in under the door, and Daniel stifled a choking cough,

"How did we let them get away with it? Forcing it all on us and telling us there was no other way. As bad as the soviets, preaching one creed and living by another. 'All pigs must obey the market, but some pigs can obey it less than others.' And all the poor, out in the dark —"

Daniel could only see one, weather-beaten face.

"— Could only swallow their anger."

Suddenly the old man quietened, breathing heavily. "And then of course, it all ended. The machine broke. *Then* there was vengeance."

— A club rising and falling, like a blacksmith's hammer working heat-softened metal —

"Destroying everyone. The dying killing the healthy, the healthy killing each other."

Daniel's breathing rasped loudly in the suddenly silent room. Carl looked down at his glass, finished his drink in a gulp and then just watched him for a moment as he struggled for breath.

"Fuck it," he muttered, standing up and shuffling to the door. "Fuck it all."

The sun shone down weakly on the rippling sea of moor grass as Daniel walked away from the cottage, following the ridge south. The weather was ideal for travel, but he could not appreciate the fresh breeze or the sublime curves of the hills. He stared back to the cottage, to Carl digging silently at the back of the cottage. Once he had seen humanity as a worthless enterprise he could live without. Now he saw it in its particulars — a friend, a home — a source of forgiveness. Someone he could help. But he'd had to leave.

Chapter 8

"What's changing? Something's different, like I've got a connection – "

Yes, something's different – you're alone again and you can't accept it. You want reasons why things have gone wrong.

"Maybe. But it's not just that."

Inventing some mystical reality won't help.

"Somewhere there must be other people."

So, it is loneliness.

"There's more to it."

You wish, you hope. Why not face it?

I want to move, yes. But if it's just loneliness, why now? I didn't feel it before.

When it was all new? When you were busy learning? Of course not. Loneliness comes when you're settled, when you've found the edges.

Old and new, past and present, rational and emotional bounced their arguments back and forth in Daniel's mind as the flames of the fire died to glowing embers. He finished the last of the fish, wiped his mouth with his hand and sat back against the rock face. Spring was advancing, and it was still not dark, although through the branches of the ash tree the sky was turning peach. Since he'd left the cottage, he'd found existence in the woods aimless, pointless. He was a man in nature again, not an animal. But the adventure had gone from that feeling. Now that it wasn't a choice, now that there was nothing else. And that pulling sensation, the need to move, had risen in him almost as soon as he had lost sight of Carl's cottage. That's what had led him into that situation with the boar – and that had changed things again. The boar had been a sign –

A sign of your need for meaning. Projecting a story onto the amorality of nature. A convenient one too —a life taken and a life spared – very convenient. Except a man for a boar is hardly an equal exchange.

"So what? I'm deluding myself. Who cares? I'm living alone in the woods! Does it matter if I'm superstitious?"

Yes, if it gets you killed.

"As if I'm likely to last out here more than a few years anyway. Mad or sane, there's not much chance for me unless I move. Would it be better to stay here miserable and rational and wait to die?"

The patterns in the embers shifted silently, red to orange and white where the breeze caught them, then black again. An owl, out of sight among the alders, called and was answered. He roused himself from his thoughts, looked quickly around. He had taken a stupid risk – lowered his guard. He saw the lengthening shadows, the darkness below the trees and a fine hanging mist over the ground. It was time to get back onto the ridge. During the day, the open hillside was too exposed – one moment on the skyline could attract unwanted attention from a great distance. So, despite the heavier going in the valleys, where marshes and flooded woodlands made progress slow, they were the only option – and he was in no hurry. But at night the danger from boar and more exotic animals became greater, and the wetter ground offered few places to rest.

He damped the fire with wet leaf mulch, enough to deaden the embers quickly with little smoke. Then he scraped the mulch and ash from the stone with a branch, spreading it so it disappeared into the tilth of the forest floor, before replacing his makeshift hearth where he had found it. He picked up his knapsack and moved quickly away from the river, heading uphill until alder turned to more open, cavernous atriums of beech, and from there through blackthorn and bramble scrub to the gorse-peppered flanks of the valley. He climbed far enough that he could gaze out above the trees to see the river, gold and flashing in the setting sun, curving away from the hills. There he found a place where broken-down walls marked a ruined barn, with another ash tree, bark as pale as stone sprouting from the shell of the building. From here he could view the woodland-edge unseen, and banks of gorse would cover him if he needed to retreat. He could sleep between the western wall and the tree and be well hidden, while holes in the wall provided lookouts over the surrounding land; it was a good place to stop. Settling on the bracken-softened ground he slipped into a light sleep, as the last vestiges of sunlight faded over the woods below. The silhouette of the ash on the wall beside him was met by, and merged into, the darkness of the stone.

At some stage of the night, he experienced that partial surfacing from sleep that allows only the absorption of a brief image or impression, before torpor again overwhelms, without ever having really lost its grip. The star-scape above him was broken and smudged by clouds that were in turn dark, then grey-silver where they caught the milky beams of a waxing moon. Below, at the edge of the wood, still amongst the outer trees, he saw a white horse, its outline striped black by the tree trunks it stood between. And as it turned its head, he saw a finer, smoother reflection of the moonlight – a stripe that narrowed to a point – a single, slender spike. And then the revealed vision was obscured once more as the moon retreated behind a mass of cloud. Sleep rose once more to shroud his vision, so that the scene remained in his mind as an experience at the edge of consciousness, its reality uncertain.

He awoke as the sun rose above the walls of the old barn, sending its strengthening rays between the branches of the ash to play across his face; sometimes diamond sharp, sometimes yellow-green through the leaves. It was already warm, although mist drifted over the woods below. There was a quiet sense of coolness in the dark space under the canopy of trees where (perhaps?) he had seen – whatever it had been. He should move.

∗

To the west, a plain stretched from north to south, and into it the river meandered. But to the east the uplands continued, a spine of moorland and mountain that could shelter him for many miles before he was forced down into the remnants of civilisation. So, he headed south east, topping the ridge on which he had rested and descending into the next valley, steep and forested; regimented lines of Sitka Spruce filling the slopes. It was dark under the canopy, and silent, any sound from outside deadened by the trees and the thick coating of fallen needles that were soft beneath his feet. Progress was slow; the trees were planted close and Daniel was forced to break off countless brittle, dead branches that criss-crossed his path.

Eventually he reached a fire-break and could walk on springy mounds of grass and heather, hummocks of sphagnum and spiky stands of rushes where the ground was wet. Silver-barked mountain ash stretched and twisted towards the thin band of light between the conifers, lichen thick on their branches. In a couple of places broken down walls had subsided into the thick grass, remnants of farmsteads and field boundaries that had made way for the marching ranks of this evergreen harvest, now itself a remnant of the past. The ride contoured the valley, gently descending, and Daniel was happy to follow its course. The sun was gently fading into a thickening mist. Apart from him, nothing moved. He enjoyed the clean, sharp scent of resin in the air, the opening inflorescences of bog asphodel yellow by pools of black water, the delicate radiating fronds of the sundew's traps that appeared to be tipped with glass, red-edged like miniature Martian invaders.

Now the fire break dropped steeply, to join a wider trail below. This muddy track hugged the base of a slope that was sheer in places. It traced the route of what appeared to be an old railway line that must have been carved out of the valley side more than a hundred years before.

The deep mud on the track made him wary; it signalled recent activity – from the way the ground was poached, heavily laden horses must have been along the route, and the flat, linear furrows suggested logs been dragged from the forest to the north. But at present the way was empty, and he would have to detour many miles back up the gorge to find another path south. He decided to take the risk and follow the road. On the side opposite the cliffs, deep woodland fell away vertiginously, and he could hear a river, out of sight and some way below him. The thick vegetation would offer cover if he chanced to meet anyone, and with luck the valley would soon widen out and give him more options. A thin rain fell, pattering off the foliage of the trees. Water ran down the shining cliff face above, suggesting a heavier downpour on the hilltops, and he guessed that any pack animal or cart would be quickly bogged down if it tried to make it down the track today. Still, he stayed close to the forest, walking on a verge that had been roughly cleared by hand.

The rush of water below and the sound of rain on leaves were the only noises disturbing the stillness of the pass. Clouds, low and heavy on the hills enclosed him and the trees and the rocks and the mud. The cliffs amplified any noise and bounced it back out across the gorge, and it seemed to Daniel that his progress was broadcast for miles around, despite his attempts to move quietly. But in the end, it was those natural acoustics that saved him. He came to a place where a rock-fall had forced the track outwards in a tortuous, tight meander that blocked his view ahead. As he came close his straining ears caught a faint rhythmic splashing from beyond the bend; unmistakably the sound of footsteps – at least three people, he reckoned.

Get off the path.

He pushed his way into the undergrowth. Now he could hear voices, and close. In his haste, he was careless – looking anxiously back towards the track he did not notice that the trees hung out over a fern-covered cliff, broken by slopes of sedge, tumbling down to the river below. His last step took him onto a rounded lip of turf that subsided instantly under his feet, pitching him forward. He reached out for a branch, but it was wet with rain and slipped out of his grasp. He felt the emptiness of falling in the pit of his stomach, and although occasional beds of grass converted his descent from deadly to merely painful, they were not enough to stop him. Branches and trailing arms of bramble cut and scratched at him as he fell. Finally, rebounding off an outcrop a few feet above the river, he plunged into the freezing water. Luckily it was deep; he had fallen on the outside of a bend where the water bit into the soil and rock of the cliffs above and the currents ploughed into the riverbed – on the other side he would have been dashed against the boulders strewn in the shallows.

The river was in spate, swelled by the rain to a torrent of muddy water that dragged him along, disorientated and unable to do more than gasp for air as he was pushed to the surface, and to hold his breath when the water pulled him deep. He lost any sense of time or distance; there was just that slow tumble, the noise of the water, the icy cold. At one point, he had to twist his body outwards to avoid a tree that had fallen out from the bank, its snapped-off trunk like a spear that would have impaled him in a single, tearing second of pain. He was dimly aware, cast upwards for a moment, that the river was turning sharply east, still bounded by cliffs and trees clinging tenaciously to the thin soil of the slopes. It seemed darker, and he sensed a greater height of land above them – he and the river, which now seemed inseparable and indistinguishable from him. A tiny part of him, still capable of logical thought, was relieved – the torrent had taken him away from the inhabited valley. And now the flow lessened, the bed widened, and the slope diminished. To the left was scrubland – old pasture by the look of it – to the right the steep escarpment remained. He felt for the stones below him, and the current slackened enough for him to resist it. With the last of his energy he dragged himself to the bank, and the dry shingle felt as soft as cotton to his exhausted body.

When he came to, he was shaking uncontrollably with the cold. The only advantage was that his body was numbed, and he felt little pain from the cuts and bruises that covered him. A pallid sun stared myopically through the mist; the valley now ran east-west, and there was a path for its light between the shoulders of the hills. He needed

93

to find somewhere warm to rest, and quickly. To have survived what he had just been through without serious injury was some kind of miracle.

No good if you die of hypothermia though. Get up.

Painfully, he pulled himself to his feet and looked down the valley.

The fields by the river were narrow, tracing the course of the water, and behind them were tall, dark Douglas Firs; a mature evergreen wood that drifted up the far side of the narrow vale, receding into the mist. To the east, a high wall straddled the meadows. A gate was set into it, and it was intact. People again. But that concern was for later, now he only saw opportunity: bales of hay were stacked under a corrugated iron roof that protruded from the wall. The makeshift cover was supported by sturdy oak posts, the structure standing on a slightly raised area of land at the edge of the woods.

Just get there. Get there.

He forced himself across the grass, focused on the shelter and nothing else. His pack was sodden and heavy on his back. That he still had it was another small miracle. Each step over the rough ground was an unfolding landscape of pain, dull in his legs, searing in his right shoulder, pounding in his head, all punctuating the numbing cold that begged him to stop with wheedling persistence.

Somehow, he made it to the barn. Nothing seemed to be stirring on the other side of the gate. He crawled in between two stacks of bales, pulled handfuls of loose straw over him until he was submerged by a thick layer of the dry material. Hidden well enough, he thought –

So long as nobody comes in here.

He felt the shaking in his body begin to subside as the insulating layers around him did their work. He had cast off his pack and his sodden clothes, laying them out under the afternoon sun that was strengthening as the mist fell back. The rules of survival were deeply ingrained; even in his dazed state he had found a drying spot between barn and wall that was as well hidden from the casual passer-by as his own resting place.

When he woke it was almost dark, the threads of cloud on the horizon a sullen red above the hills, the clear sky arching above navy blue, speckled with stars. He was warm, but distracted –

Food, you need food.

He dragged himself from his hiding place, found his clothes and pack – well dried by the sun – and assessed his options.

You can't hunt at any rate.

He was stiff and aching from the trauma of the morning. There was little prospect of finding much edible vegetation; the pine forest that covered most of the valley had little understory and the pasture had been recently grazed. He foresaw a night-time trek without food and was mentally preparing himself to begin when he became aware of a sound of reassuring domestication – the clucking of chickens, close on the other side of the wall.

There might be people. Think about it.

But at that moment, there was no choice – he had to eat.

Not the gate though.

Even if it was unlocked, it would be the most exposed of entry points. Luckily, the lean-to gave him a more clandestine way in. The brickwork of the wall was rough enough to offer him some foot- and hand-holds, and by climbing at the corner where it met the stacked hay, he could gain purchase from both surfaces. His injuries slowed his movements, and he bit back a cry of pain as he eventually dragged himself onto the corrugated roof of the shelter. The top of the wall was higher than the shelter and gave him cover from anyone inside. Cautiously he peered over, and down.

Lines of furrowed ground stretched away into the dark, as far as he could make out planted up with a variety of crops. Below and to his left was a raised chicken shed – he presumed the hens he had heard were inside. Their range was confined to one corner of the area by a low chicken-wire fence, bounded by another wall. The shape of a large house blotted the sky in front, and trees were shadowy sentinels beyond it. The wall was around ten feet high, but just to his right he noticed a compost heap, piled up against the brickwork. Seeing no sign of life, he edged rightwards then turned and lowered himself (again with no little amount of pain) to hang above it. Letting go he fell into the soft warmth of rotting vegetation and, not pausing, jumped up and headed for the chicken-shed. It was very still behind the wall; just as on the track this morning the only sound was the rush of water in the river a few yards away. He reached the wire – in the dark he could barely make it out, and almost fell. He was nearly at the shed when a movement made him spin round. But his reaction was too late. Click-click. A shotgun being cocked. Before he could dive for cover, the movement he had sensed resolved itself into an indistinct figure; short and round, wearing some kind of long coat.

"Stop right where you are, sonny Jim." The figure jerked the barrel of the gun rightwards, indicating he should get out of the enclosure. He did as he was told. "Now, we're going to walk nice and slowly out of here. And you're going to meet my friend." With no other choice, Daniel walked ahead of the figure, who shuffled along behind him.

"He *will* be glad to see you," the man's rose into a laugh. "It's been a while!"

Passing through a smaller gate, they reached a cobbled yard. Opposite was a Victorian stable block and servants' quarters, and light glowed from a low window.

"In there – Harry!"

There was no response.

"HARRY."

They entered a small room with two wooden stools, a table, a bare stone floor and an oil lamp. There was a second door in the far wall. On the table stood a half-empty bottle of whisky and, incongruously, there was an easel and canvas in the corner, turned away from them. A clatter came from a back room and the inner door burst open.

"*Don't* call me Harry on these nights, you old fool; I am the *Star King.*"

"You're certainly starking," thought Daniel. Because as soon as he saw Harry it was clear he was not sane. It was not his clothes, although the flowing black cloak and purple velvet waistcoat were at best eccentric. It was not even his words. It was the clear, blue-grey eyes, behind which Daniel could almost see mangled thoughts battering around. Without pause Harry pointed at him with a long, bent finger.

"*What* is this? WHAT IS IT?" He shouted into Daniel's face, so he felt the spit fleck onto his cheek, smelt whisky-laced breath. The man with the gun seemed less certain now.

"Lord, I found it in the vegetable garden. At the chickens. I would have killed it, but given the night I thought –"

His companion stared at him for a moment as if he would fly at him in a rage, but instead sat down, abruptly on one of the stools.

"Sit." Now his voice was calm – too calm, given his entrance. There was a scrabbling noise, from down by the fire. "The rats don't like you." His eyes were fixed on Daniel. He lent forward. "They don't like you."

The fire crackled. Nobody moved. Daniel was aware that his breathing was fast and ragged, and he tried to slow it. The man noticed.

"The air too close for you in here is it, Mr Fox? Rather be out in

97

the fresh air, indulging yourself? *Gorging* yourself?"

His eyes darted from Daniel to the first man, who had sidled back to stand in the corner of the room, the gun still levelled.

"Perhaps we should let him indulge his passions, eh Briars?"

Briars nodded, his wide, booze reddened face bobbing nervously. For the first time, Daniel noticed that he was wearing the cloak of an old-fashioned magician; red with shiny gold stars stitched to it. Below it he wore threadbare tweeds and old riding boots from which his fat legs bulged as if inflated.

"Briars doesn't speak much. Which is lucky, because he's an idiot. An idiot magician. But the rats like him," he smiled and shrugged. "So, what can one do?"

Daniel neither moved nor answered.

"But you are not silent because you're stupid, Mr Fox. You're silent because you're scared of me." He bent close again "Isn't that right?"

Daniel nodded, the rats scrabbled, and the flickering light of the fire glinted in the man's eyes.

"I will do that, yes," Harry said, apparently responding to his communicants behind the skirting board. "See what he thinks."

He stood as suddenly as he had sat down, grabbed the easel and whipped it round to face Daniel. A single black line of oil paint ran from top to bottom of the canvas, straight as a die, without wobble or smudge. Aside from that the page was empty, apart from some finger marks that stood out dark towards the edges of the white expanse.

"So," the man said in his calmest, most polite voice, while his eyes roved. "What," he pranced over to Daniel and tapped him lightly on the chest, punctuating his words with that crooked finger. "Do. You. Think?"

Somehow Daniel dragged out a response: "It's striking. Simplistic

98

but full of meaning."

"'Simplistic but full of meaning'. Ha. This is my tenth attempt. Do you know why?"

"I don't."

Again, the man came uncomfortably close. "Because – I never know where to draw the line!"

He laughed, jumped back to the easel and threw the canvas onto the fire. Daniel started back, the flames blazed up, a frantic scrabbling came from behind the wall. Briars didn't move a muscle. He had seen the show before.

"On this night, you come, Mr Fox, with your pack and your knife and your adventuring ways. Over hill and down dale, Mr Fox roves. Never bothering himself about rats and paintings. And then, oh dear," the man put his hand up to his mouth. "He's caught. Trapped like a rabbit. A rabbit out of a hat. Trapped by an idiot magician. The poetry of the world is a fine weave, do you not think?"

He quaffed whisky straight from the bottle as if it was champagne and the kick did not even bring a flicker to his gaze.

"Poor, silent Mr Fox."

As he put the bottle back down on the table, a grubby plastic band was revealed round his wrist. The type – realised Daniel – worn by hospital inpatients. The man caught his gaze and his reaction; slight but obvious to so quick a mind.

"Too clever. Not like Briars; too stupid. *Too clever.*" He stood again. "Watch him." This to Briars as he strode from the room, slamming the door behind him.

Briars stood in the shadows and they all waited: Briars, Daniel and the rats. There were some crashes from the back rooms, the sound of the man moving around, perhaps searching for something. Then the air was split by a loud, drawn-out blast – the sound of a hunting horn. The door slammed back open, and the man stood in full hunting gear; red jacket, jodhpurs, riding boots and black top hat – a sword was strapped at his side. In one hand was a full glass of sherry, in the other the horn. The jodhpurs were spattered with red-brown, like a butcher's apron.

"*Run*," he whispered.

Daniel backed away, half expecting to be cut down before he could get out of the room. But the madman was in no hurry. He watched, swigged his sherry and as Daniel reached the door threw the empty glass against the wall above Briars' head, making the fat magician flinch with fear. Out in the courtyard, Daniel obeyed the instruction and ran. He tried to leave the way he'd entered with Briars, but the door was locked – Briars wasn't that stupid. Daniel could only see one other way out: a gravel path leading off from the corner of the stables into the dark beyond. Sprinting across the cobbles he reached the loose gravel of the path and nearly fell, righted himself and looked up. Beyond the stable was a long ornamental pond, with paving on each side and stone pillars supporting trellises that stretched its full length. The moon was rising, full and round above the wooded hills, and there was enough light for him to find his way. He ran alongside the pond, looking in vain for paths to the right or left. At the end a fountain sparkled in the moonlight, the water spouting from the open mouth of a painted stone lion. Behind the fountain tall, thick yew hedges drew a curtain across the garden beyond, and at their centre the face of Hermes was carved into the stonework above an ornate archway. He passed through, and for a moment it seemed that the eyes of that sculpted God glowed white as he ran beneath them.

Another hedge faced him, curving away from him with paths following its arc left and right. He took the left and ran between high, topiary walls. And then suddenly the path left the hedges behind, and he was on the edge of a lawn. At the centre of the grass a miniature temple rose, pale under the moon, with Romanesque pillars, broad steps of shining marble, and from within the sound of running water. He looked around.

Don't get cornered in there.

But there seemed no other way out: the lawn was flanked by more thick hedges, too dense to hack through in the time he had. Behind him, not far away, the hunting horn blurted. There was someone in front of him too, in the doorway of the temple – a girl – and she beckoned him urgently. He had little option but to go to her. As he mounted the steps, he saw in the dim light that she wore white robes, roman style. Her hair was platted into dark pig tails which fell over breasts not entirely obscured by her garments. She turned away from him and he entered the temple.

Inside blue-green phosphorescence lit the round chamber; steps led down into a pool that filled the room. The walls were dark blue and rough – he could not make out what they were made of. In the middle of the pool a plume of water burst up from an outcrop of carefully placed rocks, appearing to support in mid-air a gold crown that span in the jet so that the whole edifice resembled a living king of water and stone. The girl had splashed in ahead of him, her robes clinging and semi-transparent in the ethereal light. He waded in behind her; the water was cold, but warmer than the river that had transported him here, a day and another world away. Suddenly she ducked beneath the surface; there was an opening in the chamber wall, a tunnel under the water. With a kick of her legs and a ripple of her lithe body she glided through the entrance to the submerged passage and disappeared.

Daniel took a deep breath and plunged after her. With quick strokes, he reached the tunnel-mouth. Now, as he entered the narrow space, he could see what the walls were covered with – dark blue mussels, a solid mass of them. He felt a pinching sensation; he had brushed against the wall, and the shells had clamped onto the skin of his left leg. Now his arm was caught too, and the whole surface of the walls was a writhing mass of opening and closing shells, blindly trying to hold him.

Stop moving!

As he stopped, so the movement in the walls subsided, but he was still held. His lungs were bursting. He kicked with all the power he could muster, ripped his arms from the wall and put them down by his sides. Shells were ripped from the tunnel in their hundreds, some still clamped to his legs, and his blood coloured the water red in drifting clouds. But he was free. He shot forwards, kicking fast to propel himself down the tunnel. Just as he felt he couldn't hold his breath any longer, the green glow of the aquatic chamber faded. The channel opened out into a circular pond and looking up he saw the disc of the moon above the surface. He burst up into the night air.

From the silent world of water, Daniel was pitched into a frenzy of noise and light. From the pond, he looked out onto a smooth lawn, again edged by topiary hedges, archways and paths, a serpentine rill curving secretively away into the dark, the whole scene lit by burning torches affixed to posts at every boundary. The scene illuminated by their flickering light was a confusion of pleasure and horror tangled together.

The space was full of people and a band played on flutes, drums and tambourines – mesmeric, pulsing rhythms that drifted out into the crowd. And that crowd was involved in unfettered excess – couples and groups lay entwined on the turf, others rolled and splashed in the ornamental pools. Some wore pantomime heads of birds or animals; in a dark corner under a blossom tree a couple indulged their passions while a gull-headed man leered over them, drinking from an ornamental goblet. The air was full of moans and screams, pain and pleasure indistinguishable, bound together by the beat of the music, flowing as the wine flowed. One fountain seemed to run with wine and the pool around it was full of masked figures, drinking, lying semi-conscious, intertwined. Girls ran screaming from men and women with puffin masks, to be tripped or caught and fall together with indiscriminate bystanders. From the flickering shadows at the mouths of other gardens and the cries from within, it seemed that this scene was played out on many stages.

The water was warm. Beside him a girl with long blonde hair slicked back by the water bobbed to the surface, smiled and

102

wrapped her arms round his neck. She was naked. She kissed him.

"Wait, I –"

He tried to pull away, but she clung on.

"Harry won't hurt you if you stay with us. It's just his game. He drives you in here, and then all that fear turns to –" She moved her hands downwards and brought her lips close to his. "Something else".

He felt her legs wrap round his waist under the water. What the hell. He'd had enough hardship. He started to kiss her, pulling her in, and she giggled and writhed closer in his grasp. But when he looked into her eyes, they were blank. She wasn't embracing, she was clinging. He pushed away and started to clamber out of the pool.

"I'm sorry, I can't stay here."

"Have it your own way then." She pulled herself up out of the water, the curves of her body running with rivulets of water – and screamed. In a moment, the madman appeared across the lawn and his cry rose with the girl's. Daniel ran again – left, down a narrow path. Two women were locked together on a bench; the mask of one had been cast off and lay rocking on the path. A hideous goldfinch watched the two, its metallic grey beak shining in the gloom. As Daniel passed it turned and jabbed at him. He twisted aside and the barb buried itself in the arm of a man with a pheasant's head, who held a girl with dark hair that had fallen loose from its pig-tails. She was the girl who had led him into the pool. Now Daniel saw that her robe was a hospital gown.

The path turned sharply, and he ran down a long, quiet avenue, beyond the torchlight. Through the hedge in front of him drifted a cool breeze – it was the edge of the garden. He didn't have long; he took out his machete and with desperate, violent strokes hacked at the hedge, carving into the barrier. At the turn in the path the horn sounded again. Now the hunter was running towards him, sword raised. He was only metres away as the final branch fell back. Daniel

103

dived through the opening just as his pursuer lunged, the sword-blade scything down to hit the gravel where Daniel had stood only a second before. Rolling into the darkness, he found himself again at the edge of a cliff, with water rushing below. A narrow trail led off into the dark and he slipped and slid along it. The hunter scrambled through the hedge behind him, so close in his pursuit that his breath was audible.

Majestic pine trees stood over the path from the rocky slope to Daniel's right. Above them the moon and stars glittered, distant, serene. The way led up narrow steps carved from the rock, then out over a wooden bridge spanning a gorge, with only chains to hold on to. He'd made some ground on his pursuer, and it was lucky he had – he slipped on the boards, slick with mould and water.

You're going to fall.

He reached out to grab at the chains. For a second, he hung there helpless, before the footfalls of the hunter forced him with a desperate effort to haul himself back up, and to edge as fast as he could to the other side. He plunged and swerved along the trace of a path, a gulf to one side and rock to the other, finally ducking into a black tunnel filled with the sound of water. Around the bend ahead the faint glow of moonlight promised a way out, and he dashed forwards. Almost too fast: immediately beyond the turn the path simply stopped, and a wall of water fell from above into a chasm of indefinite depth. Above was open sky, but there was no way to reach it; the aperture into which the water tumbled was smoothed and wet. And now he heard Harry's rasping breath close. He turned, and there stood the hunter, gasping and sweating, but advancing, the hard light in his eyes triumphant.

"Goodbye, Mr Fox."

But Daniel turned away and let himself fall, to be immediately enveloped and pummelled down by the avalanche of water.

Chapter 9

He stood on a lawn that sloped gently down to the river, and in the trees around him Chinese lanterns were strung, illuminating a party below. As he strolled through the crowd, sipping white wine from a delicate glass he was greeted by familiar faces; friends and colleagues from the university, respectful and accepting, pleased to see him. He felt comfortable, at home; confident. A string quartet played under the trees, a buzz of conversation was punctuated by outbursts of laughter. The river reflected the lantern-light, the lights of the house, and those on the barges moored on the far bank. Now he was dancing, and his feet moved perfectly and lightly without effort, and the girl he danced with was light and perfect too. She had long dark hair in pigtails. He looked at her satin ball gown, but as he did so it changed into a gown of a different kind. The music swerved and took up a manic beat and her eyes and her laughter were insane, and they span, locked together. He turned and behind him a goldfinch with a blood red face stood over him, and its beak buried itself in his chest.

He came to, lying across a branch, the torn off end of which was jammed into his ribs. He dragged himself to his feet. Light-headed, he began to walk, away from the river and up a gentle slope. The valley was wider here than by the gardens, and the ridge he climbed had the soft feel of rolling country – the mountains and moors were behind him. The woodland was mature and there was space to move easily between the trees, through wild garlic and wood anemone that flowered in a white sea around him. Absently, he picked the garlic leaves in handfuls and ate them, and the strength of the flavour revived him slightly. Birds called all around and the air was humid. Slowly, his emptiness was filled. He felt as though nature embraced him, brought him in from the cold of the hills and the horrors of the night.

He did not know why he continued to walk, or why he chose the path he did. Badger trails criss-crossed the undergrowth, flattened vegetation marking their routes, wide, solid sett entrances dotting the slope with mounds of orange-grey soil piled industriously before them. A buzzard cried from up in the canopy and with giant wing beats flapped heavily away under the trees. Eventually he reached the place where woodland turned to scrub, and he followed the boundary on aching feet, scarcely aware of his surroundings. He climbed through bracken to the top of the ridge and looked down into the next valley.

Below, looking straight back at him, was a woman. As soon as she saw him, she beckoned. She was slightly stooped, small, wearing a thick woollen shawl against a freshening breeze, her long, straight grey hair swept back in a pony-tail. Behind her was a doorway set into the wall of a garden and beyond it a small red bricked house. His instinct was to give her, and this place a wide berth. But something about her reminded him, just for a second, of his mother – though she had been much younger when she had died. And he found himself scrambling down the slope towards her, almost against his own will. Somehow, he felt he was heading towards sanctuary. Or perhaps that was just fatigue, clouding his thoughts, urging him towards imagined comfort.

She gazed at him with sharp, grey eyes as he came up to the gateway.

"Welcome Traveller. Come inside."

Turning, she walked back into the garden, leaving the white-painted wooden door open behind her. Daniel ducked through the doorway and immediately felt the warmth of the sun radiating from the soil and from the stone of the paths, the walls holding in the heat. He followed the woman past vegetables arranged in neat rows north to south, a polytunnel, a chicken run. Too much like the place where Briars had caught him – but there was no sense of threat here. Reaching the house, she pulled open a heavy oak door, the wood greyed and gnarled, as warm as the stones in the full sunlight. Two elder trees to the left and right of the door were bent with age, but their new leaves were fresh green. He entered, and a necklace of holed stones hanging behind the door rattled gently against the wood as he closed it behind him.

Without speaking further, the woman gestured him to follow, and led him upstairs to a room with a bed. Tiredness overcame his resistance and, not noticing anything of his surroundings, he collapsed onto the sheets and was asleep almost instantly. The afternoon passed; Daniel half woke a few times, hearing only the song of a robin or the gentle sound of digging from outside where his host must be turning the soil, seeing the strip of sunlight on the wall move round with the hours. For a while, he was free from fear, completely at ease.

He dreamt of a glade and in it a Golden Man. The Golden Man looked up and saw an apple, and as he gazed at it, hungry, Daniel could see inside his head a thousand racing particles of light illuminating his translucent brain. Now the Golden Man was planning, and as he planned the form of the fruit and the tree were no longer whole, but made up of a million interlocking parts, separate and distinct from the Golden Man and from everything else, and the particles of light raced in the Golden Man's head and he moved forward and climbed the tree and did not notice it, except for the apple it held and the million parts that offered a path to what he wanted.

Daniel awoke at dusk, and the need to eat overcame the need for further sleep. He made his way back down to the kitchen. The woman was busying herself with the vegetables and herbs she had gathered from the garden. She looked up and gestured for him to sit at the old table in the centre of the kitchen.

"Share a drink with me, Traveller."

Above him were low, wooden beams blackened by smoke, and from them hung sprigs of dried herbs, a couple of hams, a brace of duck and some unidentified bundles, mysterious in the gloom of the small-windowed room. To his left a deep, wide hearth held a fire, licking at the base of a round black cooking pot. Cupboards, side boards and open shelves filled the walls, and these were lined with

107

jars of all variety of things, from preserves to objects of uncertain derivation suspended in jelly or vinegar. The woman used a heavy ladle to draw a thick, warm liquid from the pot on the fire, pouring it into two heavy mugs.

"Syllabub." She handed one of the mugs to him; the drink was thickened by creamy lumps of milk, mixed into strong, sweet sherry that he felt coursing through him immediately he tasted it. He hadn't had alcohol since the time with Carl, and he hadn't eaten for the best part of two days, except for the garlic leaves and some roots in the wood. He did not sit but stayed on his feet, close to the door.

"You needn't fear me Traveller. Though many do. I can recognise those that need help, those that should be stopped. And those that I should fear." She gazed at him.

"I'm Sylvia." Her eyes still held his and there was a sharpness and depth in her gaze.

"Daniel," he answered, but he was still ill at ease. As sleep fell back from him, the horror he had seen, entangled in his head with the face of the old man, pushed back into his consciousness. "I have to leave, I can't stay here ..."

"Because?" Still her gaze held his eyes. Then she nodded. "You don't fear me. You fear yourself. You worry what might happen, what you might do."

Like smashing someone's skull.

"Don't worry. I'm not the judge, and this is not the time for judgement. You still travel. Whatever is done can be balanced."

"You don't know – "

"It can be balanced," she repeated. "And don't worry about doing me harm. Do you think I would have survived all that," she motioned towards the window, towards the wreck of society. "If I could be hurt so easily?"

"But I can't trust myself." Perhaps he was not so different from the hunter.

"You think, I suppose, that the judgement, when it comes, will be between those with darkness within them, and those without – as if some were free of it? No, Traveller – it is what you lay up against the darkness that matters. Whether you challenge it."

There was something about her that focussed his mind – looking at her, his thoughts were quietened. He didn't answer her for a while; his ideas were confused, this reality entwined with the reality of last night, his own devils entwined with those outside. Sylvia did not rush him; perhaps his appearance betrayed the fears crowding his memory.

"I'm sorry – yesterday, last night – were not good."

"You came from the north," her brow furrowed. "Through Alston?"

"I don't know any names, but I never want to see it again."

"Then you came through Alston. And in that case, you were strong to leave it again."

"There were two men. One called Harry," he shook his head, unable to believe it had really happened.

"I'm afraid it was real." She sat down at the table and looked away, out of the window, at the hill beyond the garden walls. He sat too. "Alston was a secure hospital, before the end. Afterwards, nobody that was left wanted to go near it. Thankfully it's remote – and a landslide took away the only road three winters ago."

"Yes, they had wrist bands – some of the – and hospital gowns." He didn't feel able to tell her what they had been doing.

"If you met Harry, you were lucky to escape." She took his mug and refilled it from the saucepan. "Harry Linton – killed his family maybe ten years ago." She passed the mug back. "He was always very intelligent. But his darkness had claimed him."

"He would have killed me." He remembered the enjoyment in

Harry's eyes – the enjoyment of power. The enjoyment of fear. An enjoyment he knew himself.

Sylvia looked at him. "Traveller – Daniel. You need have no concern for death. But what he would have done to you ..."

She paused, as if uncertain whether to say more. "If, and it's a small chance, but if you should see him again," she put her hand on his. "Don't try to face him. You must run and keep running."

The possibility that this man might continue to hunt him had not occurred to him. Sylvia caught the look in his eyes. "I'm sorry. I shouldn't have said that. There's not much chance that he'd follow you. I've no reason to think he would."

That was worrying enough, but there was something else unsettling. "Why do you call me Traveller?"

"Because that's what you are – though, perhaps, you haven't understood it yet. But you have realised what you must do, at least in part, and you are open to your calling. These things I can see. You must keep moving, keep travelling."

"That's what you are?" How does she know?

Suddenly the desire to leave, to get out and away from this place rose up again. But he didn't, just as he hadn't walked away when she had beckoned him down from the hill. He was tired of holding all this to himself, of being entirely responsible. Why not answer? Why not listen? What did it matter?

"Yes, I've felt an impulse to travel. But I'm sure there's something else. It's as if – things are changing. As if I'm changing."

You'll end up like those nutters.

"I'm afraid of losing control."

Of losing control again, you mean?

He saw that Sylvia understood. Her stare never lost its intensity as they spoke, but it felt natural, not discomforting. He wondered if

110

she needed to speak at all.

"Since the End I've relied on instinct – there's no time to think." He drank more of the syllabub to take the edge from his thoughts. Sylvia was silent. "My reason is being overwhelmed."

"Maybe," Sylvia stood up. "But maybe that's not the problem. Come and look at this."

She made her way to the door, and he followed her. Outside was a jar, and there were two shapes lying still inside it. She shook them out onto the paving slabs. Two mice lay on the stones next to each other, their limbs frozen in death. The top of the skull of one of them had been bitten off, leaving a fleshy hole in its head. And the other mouse had blood over its face and on its paws.

"I found them this morning. The jar was just by the path there – they must have been chasing each other, and then fell off the boarding and got trapped." She scooped the bodies of the mice back into the jar, took a trowel and wandered up the garden to an unkempt patch of earth near the wall. Digging a small hole, she dropped the grizzly contents of the bottle into it. "Mice fight," she said as she filled in the hole. "But not to the death."

Daniel nodded. "Of course – the weaker one always retreats – dying in a fight cuts off your chances of producing off-spring, so the instinct to flee evolves."

"So?"

"So? What do you mean? In the end you get an evolved balance – between the instinct to fight and the instinct to run away."

"But in this jar, there was nowhere to escape to. They were in an unnatural situation – the victor couldn't make the loser leave, so it killed it. Then died from the stress of the fight or just the cold."

"But what's that got to do with me?"

The shadows were long. Somewhere a blackbird was singing. Sylvia led him back inside and they sat down again.

"In nature each animal can follow its instinct. Like you say, those instincts balance each other. Every individual follows the most urgent instinct they feel until it's sated, or another becomes more important, and then it switches to the next. It all fits, it all works. Animals just act. They can't unbalance things. But we can. We make the jars."

"That's very neat but what about all the extremes in nature? Chimps murdering each other? Orcas playing with the bodies of seals? How does that fit with your natural balance?"

"You make a good point," she nodded. "I do tend to sanitise the description a bit. Balance between instincts doesn't mean no extremes. As you say, evolution produces some horrific solutions, like fly larvae eating caterpillars from the inside out. The point is, in nature those solutions evolved for a reason. We create *un*natural conditions. And because they're unnatural, evolved instincts drive behaviour that might not be in the interests of the individual – because they're in a situation beyond what their instincts were evolved to deal with. That's the imbalance we bring."

"I still don't get what you mean. We're animals too, just another species. OK, we do damaging things – but that's because we lived in societies that were nothing like the environment we evolved in. Our instincts weren't in step with the modern world."

"Well, exactly, that's the point – we have the ability to transform things so much that we put *ourselves* in conditions we weren't adapted to. More than that though. You can't say that our wickedness is just down to modern living, can you? I think you've found out that going back to nature doesn't change things, haven't you? That we still end up doing disproportionate things?"

Daniel gripped his mug so hard that his knuckles whitened. Sylvia carried on. "Human beings can't just live like animals. We can't find that balance that nature has. Even when we've given up on being human."

"Stop!"

112

"You know your journey isn't a normal one Daniel. Will you be open to where it takes you? Or will you run?"

"You can't ..." Nothing made sense.

Sylvia paused and placed her hands over his on the mug. "Ok, I'm sorry. You must feel very lost. But you have to keep going, despite that."

Daniel's head swam with fatigue and alcohol. Sylvia re-filled his mug – but with water this time – and cut a home-made cob into thick slices. Then she brought a block of yellow cheese from a larder at the back of the room, as well as a knife and a slab of butter. Amongst Daniel's swirling thoughts, the question of how she'd made those things, and from what, arose only briefly.

"You need to focus, Traveller – Daniel. The point is, all of us are out of sync, all of us are capable of extremes. Not just you. The question is, why? What is it that makes it impossible to find the balance that we see in nature?"

An image of Adam and Eve with their fig leaves came into Daniel's mind. He forced himself to find an answer. "We can think – reason," he said, eventually. "That's the difference, obviously – how we can make changes so quickly that evolution can't keep up, how we unbalance things."

"But reasoning is just a tool, isn't it? Logical thought is just a type of natural selection but with ideas instead of genes – you choose X over Y because you expect it'll help you get something you want. You have to go deeper than that. What allows us to reason? What is it that doesn't let us stop?"

Suddenly, Daniel had had enough. "This is crazy. Look outside. You expect me to start philosophising in the middle of this?"

Sylvia just smiled. "You know you need to travel. Perhaps this is part of your journey. What is it that makes us different? What is it that separates us from everything else?" She held up her hand as he started to speak. "I know, I'm pushing you too hard, Traveller. You need to sleep. And I'm afraid that after that you have to move on

113

again. But just remember, there is an answer."

Without waiting for a reply, she led him again up the narrow stair of age-darkened polished oak, sloping and uneven. He hadn't noticed them when he first arrived, dead tired, but now, though groggy with the syllabub and the confusion of that conversation, he took in the framed copies of woodcuts that hung on the walls, his mind fixing itself on their solid familiarity, a line trailed out over a rough sea. There was a plough and horse working a field edged by copses of tall, sweeping elms, pastures and woods, a flock of grazing sheep watched over by a shepherd with staff and smock on high down land. A low window on the landing gave a view of the darkened garden and the trees beyond, ghostly under the moon, and a charm of feathers and crystals hung from the window latch. Sylvia carried a candle in a glass. Entering the low-ceiling room in which he had slept earlier, she used her light to feed a candle that stood on an ornamental dresser and left him without a word.

For once the enclosed space seemed to be protective rather than oppressive. An open window let in the cool night air and the voices of the owls. Despite, or perhaps because of his sense of disorientation, he fell asleep quickly, under a quilt whose patches carried symbols of trees and spirals, depictions of birds and animals; some real, some mythical. He had a vivid dream – or did he wake? In it he crossed the darkened room and gazed out over the garden. Sylvia was outside the gate in a long, white cloak. In the gloom beneath the trees, she fell forward onto all fours and, struck by the moonlight, her form became that of the unicorn. And she disappeared into the dark, and the garden and the scrubland below were still and silent. Looking beyond, far to the south west, a star stood on the horizon, brilliant white. The light spread and filled his gaze, until it became the first glow of daylight hitting his eyes through the un-curtained window. It was time for him to leave.

She was waiting for him in the hall below and walked out with him. The grass and flowers glittered with dew, their colours still pale in the dawn light. The air had a sharp edge of cold, and beyond the gate the scrub was faded by mist.

"Last night ..."

But she only laughed. "The things of the night are for the night, and now it is the day. Follow the path down a way, to where it meets the old forest ride. Your road lies south and west, but the plain is flooded – the river defences collapsed a couple of years ago – so you need to go east, along this wooded ridge. You'll get to a place where there's a road over the flatlands. It's flooded too, but the water's only shallow and the surface is firm. That way will bring you round to your true direction. If you trust your intuition the rest will be clear."

"Thanks for your advice, and for the food." His words were clumsy in the ethereal light, which seemed to glow around Sylvia and almost live, connecting her to all that was around her. She and this place were at one. She smiled and opened the small wooden gate for him to pass through.

"Goodbye Traveller – may you reach your destination safely."

*

Walking away from the house, Daniel contoured the hill following a gravelled ride, through the surface of which sprouted thin, upward-stretching ash saplings. Mist hung over the ground and the air was suffused by the warm glow of morning sunlight re-colouring the grey world of night-time. A solitary roe deer stalked across the path ahead of him, oblivious to his presence, and occasionally he heard the barked calls of others, deep among the trees. The constant competing songs of chiff chaffs, great tits, willow warblers and thrushes, was so persistent and frenetic in the spring morning as to be almost oppressive. Trees were bedecked with green, its hue varying with species to form a mosaic of shades. The leaves shrouded the smooth trunks of close-planted beech standing in rows. They lay between more natural plots of woodland where there was less order among the silver-tinted stems of coppiced hazel and the rutted, ancient oaks whose bark looked and felt like rock. Several times woodpigeons burst from overhanging branches as he was almost upon them with a flurry of heavy wing beats, rabbits scattered from the verges, and he passed areas of nuzzled brown earth where boar had been foraging.

The ride led him gently downhill. Gazing out over the willow scrub at the wood's edge he saw the wide plain that Sylvia had told him about. To the north a river glinted along its meandering length. It was defined only by edgings of banked earth and distant lines of poplar, for as she'd said, the fields wore a cloak of water speckled with protruding beds of rushes, hemmed by the remains of human boundaries, houses marooned on a plate of silver that reflected the rounded, grey clouds and the pale blue of an empty sky. Again, as Sylvia had predicted, this landscape was passable; the seasonal floods lay upon good ground, not treacherous marsh. Following the old lane she'd told him about, the flood rarely reached his knees although, wary of hidden hazards beneath the surface, his progress was slow.

Ripples spread in his wake and ran out ahead of him, furrowing the mirror-world below. Was it the Celts that had believed that pools were windows, gateways into a magical other-place? As he walked, reality seemed ephemeral. Below his feet ancient warriors strode a land untouched by the scars that cut so deep in this. But his tread shattered his view of that place, and he passed through the land of the dead but was separated from it.

In time, he came to a place where the ground was artificially banked; a broken-down fence divided the scrubby fields from dense woodland made up of an artificial mix of species: Norwegian maple, alder, mountain ash and an occasional Scot's pine. The bank stretched in either direction in a gentle curve. The landscaping, the glimpses he had of metal gantries and, about half a mile away where the bank was devoid of trees, the concrete arch of a bridge, showed him it was a motorway. He would have to cross it, which felt risky – he would be exposed to anyone on the road for a mile or so in either direction. Irrational of course – there was no more reason for anyone to be there than anywhere else.

The fence was a simple wooden affair; under the overhanging branches of the trees it was slick with mould and mostly rotten. Instead of climbing it he just pulled the top bar back from a post and stepped through, to hack through the undergrowth of this un-grazed space. Squirrels chattered and scrabbled among the low branches at his intrusion, and a woodpecker broke away from the canopy and headed out over the scrub and the grey water with a dipping flight.

Eventually he reached the crest of the ridge and stared down at the highway. He stood there for a long while, unmoving. Grass and moss were encroaching on the carriageways, giving an odd piebald look to the road, and along the central reservation thickets of birch and ash had pushed through the gravel. It was still down there between the wooded banks, the trees like a crowd gathered in an amphitheatre, watching the show below.

Along the carriageway closest to him, vehicles were crushed and thrown together. They formed contorted shapes, like a rubbish tip for sculptures discarded by some deranged artist. A lorry lay on its side, burnt out and blackened, a dam behind which cars and vans jostled, some overturned, one half through the Armco barrier in the centre of the road.

Before the End, he had turned off the news every time car accidents were mentioned. While other people rubber-necked at road accidents he avoided even a glimpse. The feeling that he had left his parents like this, had moved on without them, flowed over him once more. That guilt he'd explained away so eagerly in the first flush of his enchantment with evolutionary theory. He scrambled down the bank and onto the tarmac, walking through the wreckage with no thought anymore of his exposed position. Personal belongings were scattered: the ragged remains of clothing, a rusting electric razor, a jar of face cream. He imagined them being hastily collected together in a last attempt to escape. But better this maybe, than the waiting and the Instructions and what came next.

His eyes ran over the detail of structure crumpled and deformed, order smashed into chaos. He could almost hear the impacts, the screams of the trapped. Here, the front of a car had been concertinaed, ramming the dashboard back into the cab with the weight of the engine behind it. Some clothing remained, tattered in the tangled space. There were a few broken pieces of bone, most having been carried off by animals, those remaining pieces cleaned with keen efficiency by a myriad of organisms.

As he stared, a robin darted into the wreck. It looked at him for a second, head on one side. Then, standing on the steering wheel, it began to sing. He stood transfixed by the flow of those notes, their rise and fall, their melody. He could not have said how long he stood and listened as that song echoed around the cutting. The music bound connections that had been broken long ago. The same facts, the same history, the same present were re-ordered. He wasn't standing among the dead. These were only husks, artefacts, disintegrating while the humanity they had carried had vanished in a second. Or at least changed in a second. Surely all that meaning couldn't just stop so suddenly? Now that was a thought from the past. A belief. The sun shifted behind a veil of smoke-like cloud. He scrambled up the far embankment with a new eagerness for his journey, the song of the robin still echoing behind him.

Chapter 10

A day later, out on the plain, amid the soft green of trees that were tiny alongside it, he came upon the bowl of a radio telescope. It lay at an angle, the geometry of its underpinnings twisted and disjointed. One of the two scaffolding pillars that supported it had buckled, so that the bowl was only partly suspended. Its face, once brilliant white to prevent its panels warping in the sunlight, was stained and peppered with moss where mud had collected in tiny crevices between each section of steel sheet. Brooding clouds piled high across the sky behind it. Nature cycled as this leviathan fell apart in gradual stages and occasional catastrophic collapses; rusting metal bolts, struts and mechanisms giving way to the force of the wind, the insipid action of water.

Daniel was drawn to this wreck. He climbed up the frame of metal beams, onto the rim of the dish where it had wedged itself into the earth, crushing trees beneath it. Up here, even the weak sunlight that pierced the clouds was enough, once reflected off the curving metal, to provide some warmth. The size of the dish, its precision, were such that he looked round at it continually, tried and failed to capture its form. What would it take to build another like it? Where would you start? Miners extracting the metals, factories turning out components, builders, machinery. Beyond them, the builders and maintainers of that machinery, the farmers and supply chain that provided food to everyone constructing it, the doctors keeping them healthy, the teachers helping them gain their skills. Each individual reliant on a whole host of others, and them in turn reliant on more. Not so obvious when you had money in your pocket. Free as a bird – like he'd been – master of his own destiny. Until you found out what it was to be alone. He looked at his pack, his patched clothes. Still, he was reliant on what others had made.

What am I?

The shadow of the telescope stretched out across the trees and scrubland. Daniel lay back and drifted to sleep in the warmth of the sun. He was playing cards with Sylvia – she dealt, just one card. He turned it over. The Queen of Diamonds. And then that scene vanished, and he was looking over a grassy plain, scattered with trees and bushes. There, tethered to a post, was an ape. It was on safe, soft grass but beyond the length of its rope were bushes full of berries, heavily laden fruit trees. The ape tugged at the rope to reach some of the food, and it extended, just a little. It could eat a few berries. It tugged again and the rope extended again, only a few centimetres but enough that it could eat a bit more. It tugged a third time and suddenly the rope snapped. Released, the ape stretched up and ran on two feet to the nearest berries and began to eat. Behind it, in the glade it had left, a shining ladder had appeared – but the ape was focussed on eating, grabbing down more than it could swallow, pushing its way into the bush to get more. And Daniel saw a pit there and realised that the ape would fall. Suddenly he was looking through the eyes of the ape into the blackness of that pit and there was horror there.

He started up from where he lay, fully awake. For a moment he was disorientated by the curved whiteness all around him. He could only think of the dream. He steadied his breath and clambered down off the dish. As he got close to the ground, uneasiness filled Daniel as if it rose up to him from out of the earth. Walking away, he looked back over his shoulder at the telescope. What had he been thinking, sitting up there, above the trees? Exposed to anyone watching. Philosophising and forgetting where he was. Unconsciously he quickened his pace.

What if Harry is following you?

The hunter and the hunted. The blackness of a pit. He stopped himself. Those thoughts were groundless. Spiralling beliefs. That future was woven from Sylvia's words and his own fears, not from any external sign. Enough. He turned back to the present and the country around him. The land here had been pasture reclaimed over the centuries from peat bogs and heath. Now, that primeval

120

landscape was spreading again, out across what were once fresh, fertilized green rye grass and clover leys; scrubby woodlands of silver birch, bracken, bilberry and heather, alder and standing water, circling buzzards, snipe and various ducks that multiplied fast, no longer the targets of shooting parties.

He followed old lanes which had almost been overcome by brambles, grasses and weeds, between hedges grown wild and thick. Cautiously he passed farms in various stages of dilapidation: red-bricked houses with broken windows, abandoned tractors and machinery, milking parlours, concrete aprons where old layers of manure now fed eager nettles, dandelions and thistles. The silence was strange here – no distant tractor engine, fading and growing as the machine turned back and forth, mowing the grass for silage, no buzz of passing cars, no low hum of milking machines.

He was tempted to investigate some of the dwellings, intrigued by the machinery and the arrays of outbuildings that might hold tools or equipment that could be useful. But he restrained the impulse – it was not worth the risk – enough to be walking past these places, without tempting fate by venturing inside. Before the afternoon darkened to evening under the clouds, he fished in an old mill pond, catching a broad, heavy trout from the brown water. On the opposite bank, a heron paused in its own hunting and watched him. He was not sure whether its look was envious of his catch or pitying of his clumsiness. As he left, the bird – which had been gazing at the water with the air of a philosopher deep in thought – dipped its head like lightening and came out with a fish equal to his own. It was hard not to believe they'd been competing.

By the time night fell Daniel was cooking his trout over a bright fire of birch and heather, having found a patch of woodland on slightly higher ground, and therefore dry underfoot. The density of saplings and the tangle of bracken at the edge of the copse were, he hoped, enough to conceal the light of the flames from anyone passing. As the last of the colour left the sky, his meal finished, he put out the fire and slept on a bed of young bilberry and springy turf. Once he awoke, roused by a movement in the undergrowth –

but it was only a fox, wiry and lean, sniffing out the remains of the trout that he had cast away from his camp. The night remained dry but at dawn a thin rain began to fall from a sky of blank grey, and he packed his kit, starting on his way before the damp atmosphere could chill him.

As he walked, he began to pass more houses, and the first signs of old industrial development. The lane he followed joined a wider road, there was a forecourt filled with rusting cars, their sales stickers faded on the windscreens, brambles weaved over wheels and between wiper blades. The porta-cabin office was burnt out, and there must have been an explosion at the neighbouring petrol station – the canopy had half collapsed and everything close was scorched. Daniel climbed over a chain-link fence to follow a track shadowing the road – he had no desire to advertise his entry into the city by advancing along the wide, open highway. Something drew him towards the urban sprawl, and he rationalised his progress by arguing that the settlement was too expansive to skirt around. Still, the air of desolation, commercial enterprise without vendors or customers, the futility of advertising hoardings and abandoned tat, depressed him. Such places had held little enough character when people teemed in the showrooms, ate in the car parks of the now smashed in drive-thrus, wasted weekends in the corrugated metal and concrete caverns of DIY stores and electrical outlets. Now empty, their pointlessness was emphasized, these atriums of exchange echoing with ghosts.

At first the urban sprawl was patchy: estates, shops and commercial buildings interspersed by overgrown fields and sodden woodland. The landscape was scaled for the car driver – stretched out along wide roads so that to Daniel it seemed he was making little ground. He edged ant-like past large car-parks, long, grim warehouses set in landscaped banality. In abstract – up in the mountains – the idea that humanity had been all but erased by disease and violence had seemed a straightforward concept – horrific but not unfathomable. Here, it was much harder to take in; there were so many things, so many houses and buildings, so many

122

cars, vans and trucks rusting along the road.

His path was not straight. Beneath its coat of concrete and brick, the land rolled in a series of low hills with wide vales between them. These lower areas were inundated with flood water. Just like out on the plain the defences here must have quickly deteriorated without repair or maintenance, and he was forced to skirt these bleakly unimaginative Venetian scenes. Church spires, chimneys and high-rise flats – often listing dangerously, their foundations eroding – poked up from the water like the fingers of drowning men, and only flocks of wheeling gulls broke the silence with their cries.

He carried a short broken off piece of scaffolding pole to defend himself. Not from people – his machete could deter them – but from animals. Dogs could be a threat here. But, in fact, he saw few: a bedraggled mongrel stalking across wasteland in the distance and, more menacingly, a growling Alsatian, thankfully separated from him by a swollen stream. He guessed many pets might simply have died without their owners or, perhaps they were rounded-up and killed as potential vectors of disease, in the panic of the End.

Death was intimated by every absent sound, every empty building, every unmoving car. It was explicit in the piles of body bags at a cemetery gate (long since split open, their contents devoured by rats and other creatures) but crept more insidiously into Daniel's mind when suggested by weeds scrambling over deserted schoolyards and play areas.

This had been a large conurbation, joining many towns and villages in repeating waves of growth – industrial parks gave way to estates, estates to terraces and shopping streets, shopping streets back to estates and industrial parks. Although he was not yet in the heart of the city, the open land of a municipal park gave him a longer view; he made out office blocks in the distance, and a little to one side of them the pale thrust of a cathedral tower. His parents and God jutted upwards on the skyline of his mind.

The cathedral pulled at him but, at the same time, he felt that something wasn't right with it, just like when, years ago he'd looked

123

across at that garage in the glacial valley with the machine oil sign and the broken-down car inside. There was a sense of darkness that was more than the shades of past horror that shrouded the rest of this place. But his path lay that way.

It was mid-afternoon as he came to the proper centre of the city. The height of the buildings increased, flats stacked up above shops – large apartment stores and clothes outlets – and ahead the tower and ornate turrets of the cathedral, rising above the clutter of modernity with proud resilience. He approached slowly, somehow unable to resist looking closer, fearful and yet entranced by it. Signs of damage became more apparent. Most of its windows were smashed out, a fire had scarred one side, and the roof was caved in in several places. To him, despite his rejection of religion, it was distinct from that sea of development he'd crossed to reach this place. It marked continuity while the relics surrounding it spoke of instability and ephemeral power.

One of the heavy doors guarding the north entrance had been ripped out, the other damaged. Stepping inside he felt, still, the change of atmosphere, the contrast between the outer world and a place of prayer, even though this one was now only a shell. He stood on the expanse of smoothed stone flags and gazed down the central aisle. Above him – far above – a hole rent in the roof let in a stream of light, a trickle of water and hanging tendrils of ivy. The last time he had been inside a church had been for his parents' funeral. Them encased in the polished wooden boxes at the altar rails. When he'd asked God why and found the answer in the silence.

Stone columns towered left and right along the nave from the smashed-out rose window behind him, to the altar in front. Wooden fixtures – pews, lecterns, the rood screen – had long since been taken for firewood. Walking forward he saw a more ideological violence: a freshly mutilated statue of a saint, its head absent. Medieval wall paintings, lovingly restored before the End, were crudely scratched out, carvings of angels hacked into, removing their faces. As he wandered amongst the broken remains, the silence was

124

pierced by shouts from outside. He ran across the cathedral, into the north wing of the transept, out of view of the shattered opening of the main door. Something, perhaps a mortar, had long ago torn a gap in the stonework here. From this aperture, by climbing up over the rubble surrounding the exit wound, he could look out unseen.

In what had once been the carefully tended grounds of the cathedral – wide tarmac paths, benches, wrought iron lamp posts, parkland trees – there was a large, uneven circle of bare, packed earth, kept free of grass and weeds by repeated use. Most of the lampposts had been taken for their metal, and the trees for wood, their uneven stumps black against a backdrop of ruined offices and apartments. In the circle was a pile of rocks and stones; the broken fragments of the saints and angels whose other remains still littered the church.

The sense of something wrong coalesced here. The shouting was coming from a mob slowly making its way into the churchyard, past the tree stumps and towards the circle. The crowd was made up of around forty men, young and old. At the centre of it, a young woman was being dragged along. The men picked up shards of stone from the pile and gathered round the prone woman. Their actions were like those of machines; they followed instructions, empty-eyed.

As he watched, the first man – lean, tall, strong – strode up to the woman, a girl really, with dark hair and frightened eyes, and hurled a chunk of rock at her head. It hit with a horrible crack and knocked her to one side. Then another stone thudded against her back. Another and another landed on her. She could not protect her face any more. Part of the stone wing of an angel ripped open her cheek. Daniel stared. It went on and on. Then they stopped and drew back. The girl lay amid stones stained by blood and flesh. Someone stepped forward, knelt by her and held her wrist. He was checking her pulse. They had to be sure she was dead before they would stop. As the stones began to be thrown again, Daniel turned away. He ran across the cathedral to an opening in the far wall, past a dried-up font with a fissure that ran from edge to edge and

125

stumbled out into the park. He ran without any awareness of what was around him. Apart from the sound of his progress, silence hung over the wrecked city.

Later, he found a place to shelter for the night. It might have been more secure to rest up in one of the countless ruined buildings, but he didn't. He wanted to be outside. Before, that desire had come from feeling like an imposter in those places – they had been homes and businesses, now they were a space for ghosts, still full of the echo of death. But this time he just wanted space to breathe. He holed-up in an overgrown town house garden, beneath an apple tree. The spot was bounded by dense shrubs that kept him hidden, and a high, brick garden wall. He lay for many hours on the rough ground, the scene he had just witnessed churning around in his mind. He was part of that horror, trapped by belief. Eventually as a thin, pale dawn lightened the sky above the roof-tops, he slept.

It was mid-morning when he was disturbed by the screeches of two tom cats fighting. They were close, and he got up and quickly packed his blanket. With no access to antibiotics, being bitten was a potential death sentence. He continued west – there didn't seem anything else to do. His preference for alleys and gardens over the exposed main roads slowed his pace and he was tired and on edge, uncertain in this wrecked artificial setting.

Every scene evoked destruction: a rusting metal advertising board outside the remains of a newsagents promising ice-cream for sale, a teddy bear propped up in the gutter like a beggar beside a pavement torn apart by the upward thrust of a large, leggy buddleia, a burnt-out chip shop, its high counter like an iceberg in a sea of smashed glass and brickwork, one end warped and melted.

As the afternoon wore on, he thought he might pass the day without seeing anyone. But that was wishful thinking. A collapsed building forced him from the weed-infested back street he had been following, and he emerged onto a dual carriageway. A rusting bus blocked the near lanes. Again, rats had long-since cleansed the scene. Only the shadow of it remained. He was about to cross to the relative safety of a stand of thick shrubs – a previously well-manicured municipal display – when he saw, in the distance, about a dozen people advancing down the road, walking in two rough lines. They carried an assortment of clubs and other improvised weapons. Luckily, they were focussed on scanning the buildings close to them and hadn't noticed him in the shadows at the edge of the path.

He had to hide, and somewhere close. He looked around. The building behind him was relatively intact, at least in its basic structure; a concrete block of four or five storeys. From its appearance, he guessed it might have been a university department. It was easy to enter – the ground level had originally been walled by floor-to-ceiling panes of glass that were long gone – and he slipped inside. The stairway looked solid, and he sprinted up it, with light, silent strides.

At the head of the stairs were fire doors, intact. He opened them carefully and passed through, finding himself at the head of a long corridor with doors leading off on both sides. He ran half its length, picked a door and with as much caution as his haste would allow, pushed into the room. It was, thankfully, empty; or rather it was littered with a miscellany of lab equipment but there was nobody there. The windows were unbroken – he realised they were made of reinforced glass – and keeping low he moved between formica work benches to peer out at the street.

Suddenly, the focus of his senses shifted from the scene outside to the very intimate space of the room he occupied. From the next room, he had heard a squeaking sound. Now there was a rattle, like someone moving an office chair or a trolley. He stood completely motionless as the door connecting this lab to the next swung open. It was an obsolete strategy – he was in plain sight of the man who scurried in. The slight figure glanced up, saw Daniel and to his surprise paid him no attention. Instead, the man busied himself at a workbench, beginning to pipette a clear liquid into a row of capillary tubes with a plastic syringe. He wore white latex gloves and despite his air of anxiety his hands were steady as he worked. He must have been in his forties, with dark-framed glasses, a pale angular face with sharply defined features that, Daniel guessed, were more the result of a lack of food than a natural attribute. Where, he wondered, did the man get his lab supplies? And how had he survived in here alone? He corrected himself – apparently alone.

"Excuse me."

But the scientist seemed oblivious to his existence; he tried again, moving closer and speaking more loudly. "Excuse me."

Now the man looked up, apparently taking in his presence for the first time. "You've come for the results I suppose? Well, they aren't ready, not yet. I have to be sure; a few more tests, then we'll see." He turned back to his task. "Why can't you give me time?"

Daniel started to explain, but the man, who had apparently finished what he was doing, hurried back out of the lab without looking up. Daniel followed him to the door. But when he looked inside there was no-one and nothing there. The room was bare, only the fixed shelving remained. Looking behind him, the room he had just left was the same. He ran to the door and along the corridor, down a fire escape. But this was reality. There wasn't anywhere normal to run to. Outside again, along an alley away from the main street, he walked on towards the west.

Horror, emptiness. Sylvia's ideas like riddles. He still couldn't see what it was that set humanity apart from nature. Maybe she was wrong. Maybe there was nothing. To his left, a few ducks drifted on a pond of muddy water that had filled the foundation ditches of a building site. Startled at the sight of him, they began a heavy, clumsy surge across the water, until finally they broke away to slide upwards between the buildings, wings whirring. And his brain whirred with those wing beats. Breaking away. A threshold. A rope snapping. An ape standing. The playing card – the Queen of Diamonds. Of course. He laughed out loud. Just what he'd been telling those undergraduates about at that party in another time and another world. An arms race, and its direction taking a species over a physical boundary. Taking the human brain over a boundary. And if the brain gained a new capacity, if the mind transformed? Then

128

gradually evolved instincts would be like police officers on bicycles chasing a stolen Porsche. Out of step. Evolved to regulate a brain without the new capability, untested and unqualified to direct one that now, suddenly, worked differently. No rule book, no map. No way out.

Chapter 11

Low cloud lay over the ruined city and now darkness fell quickly. This place that once lit the sky with the glow of its life held a blackness more complete than that of any forest, and the debris choking its alleyways and side streets was more obstructive and treacherous than the most tangled briar patch. Occasionally Daniel heard distant shouting or saw through broken windows the orange flicker of fires. Humanity lost in the night. A sense of futility overwhelmed him. Finally, he slumped against a concrete wall that was now a monolith, separated by violence and decay from its role as part of a building, part of something with a meaning. One side of it still had a large photograph attached to it, a mouldy sofa clutched at its base. A memory of inside, of protection.

Time passed. A haze of rain blurred even those rough silhouettes of buildings still visible in the dark, gave a physical shape to the disintegrating force of time. The cold began to soften his senses and he felt he had no energy left to fight it. His mind drifted.

The Golden man span slowly against the stars. Or maybe he was still, and it was the stars that span. The particles of light that coursed through him reached out through the tips of his fingers and from his feet and from his eyes but the stars could not receive them, and they could not escape his body.

Daniel half surfaced from the dream. Had he been here for seconds or hours? It didn't matter. Suddenly, there was a clatter of dislodged lumps of masonry behind him. In the rubble, something moved with more purpose than the decaying rain. He heard shallow breathing close in the damp night air.

"Traveller."

The whispered voice was close.

"Traveller."

He turned his head and saw a figure amid the tangle of the night.

It was a boy, perhaps twelve or thirteen. The boy beckoned:

"Come this way, *quickly.*"

It was probably a trap. But why fight fate anymore? Why not follow? Perhaps this child was taking his soul, releasing him. As he stood, he wondered if, behind him in the dark, his body still lay in the debris.

The boy moved quickly, instinctively, and Daniel struggled to keep up. After a few minutes, he'd lost all sense of direction. He could only follow his guide's shadowy form, blindly trusting this strange child. At last, the boy stopped, where a rusted metal door stood wedged ajar, leaving just enough space for them to squeeze through into a pitch-black space beyond. The child fumbled at something on the ground, moved aside a piece of corrugated iron to reveal a hidden door, a hatch set in concrete.

"You can come inside and warm up."

"Why –?"

"You're a Traveller. There are rules though: You can eat and drink as much as you like, and you can stay for the night. But afterwards, you must move on. Don't speak while you're with my parents – they won't answer you. I'll make sure you get everything you need."

"But who are you? Why –?"

"Just a family. We must all help the Travellers." Daniel opened his mouth, but the boy stopped him –

"Your road will show you what you need to know. This is just a resting place – the journey is your own."

With surprising strength, the boy pulled open the hatch and they descended a short flight of steps with another door at its foot. He lit a candle that sat in an alcove and quickly reached back and brought the hatch down behind them with a thud. All the sounds of the night, the soughing wind, the almost imperceptible patter of rain, were cut off. The flickering light was barely enough for the boy to fit the key he produced from the pocket of his thick, home-made trousers into the door lock.

"Remember – don't speak."

The door swung open at his guide's touch, and they stood at the threshold of a small, cluttered kitchen. A woman, in overalls brightened incongruously by a red shawl, stood stirring a large pan of stew, and the air was rich with the warm smells of herbs and animal fat. Candles burned within hurricane lanterns casting an uneven light through the room.

"A Traveller is here." The boy announced, his voice formal.

The woman turned with a start, and for a second her expression seemed to Daniel to be one of fear. But she collected herself quickly, and smiled, at least with her mouth.

"John!" She called. "Dominic has brought a Traveller."

Dominic waved Daniel forward into the room, pulled the door shut behind them and locked it.

"Don't worry mum."

"Where should he sit?"

"At the head of the table." The boy pulled out a chair – "Here, Traveller."

He sat. The woman did not look at him but turned back to the stew, which she began ladling into rough wooden bowls. A man came through from another room, ducking beneath the low concrete doorframe. Daniel guessed this had been a bunker before the End. Now the walls were lined with shelves holding cooking pots, plates and books, a selection of hanging meats which Daniel suspected were cat, some old pictures, dirty from constant exposure to steam and evaporated fat.

The man sat, glanced over at Daniel then away, like an interviewee on a TV show who has been told not to look at the camera but can't resist it. There was silence except for the sound of the food being served, the crackle of burning wood from within the range, improvised from an oil drum. A flue, pieced together from scrap metal bent and beaten into shape, led up to and filled the aperture of a ventilation duct in the ceiling, modern engineering adapted to a primitive new reality.

"Traveller, receive this food and remember us at your destination." The woman placed a bowl of stew and a spoon in front of Daniel and again spoke without looking at him.

"Relax mum," said the boy. "Travellers are just people, you know that." He turned to Daniel. "I'm sorry, they're always like this. They've met many Travellers and they're still the same. No –" This in response to Daniel opening his mouth to speak, "Just eat. This is my mum, Liz, and my dad, John."

The two murmured their hellos as if the roles of child and parent had been reversed.

The introduction seemed to help Dominic's parents act more normally. John began to eat quickly, occasionally wiping excess sauce from round his mouth where a rough beard sprouted. His face was heavily lined, although Daniel did not think he was as old as those lines suggested – there was still a youthful vigour in his blue eyes – the same striking colour as his son's.

"Is the planting going OK dad?"

"The planting's fine, and the soil in the new field's good. So long as they don't find it, we'll be fine this year."

"And Gerald?" Asked his wife.

"Ha!" Her husband exclaimed between mouthfuls. "Still lording it over us. You'd think after five years he'd give us some credit for knowing the job. But he's still the farmer and we're still the labourers. Anyway, he keeps young Gwyn in check I suppose."

"That's only going to get harder."

"He'll leave, like the others. But so long as he stays long enough for Dom here to take his place, we'll be alright."

He smiled at Dominic.

"I'll stay dad, don't worry."

There was a brief silence, then John took up his thread again.

"Anyhow, it was 'Flower' he was on at today ..."

"John, her name's Blossom!"

"Well, she was living up to her name anyway – standing looking pretty while the rest of us worked."

Daniel had thought he would never experience this human routine, this small talk, again. Especially not in this city. But here it was, civilisation springing up like a dandelion punching through the tarmac. Now his time in the mountains, his capitulation to instinct, seemed even more bestial than he had felt even with Carl. Happy and empty at once he ate and let the words and the food bring comfort.

Dominic, watching him, smiled. "The Traveller likes the stew mum."

"I'm glad."

"Anyway, talking of Flow – Blossom," John went on. "She scared herself, and us, half to death this afternoon – reckoned she saw a man watching us work, up in one of the ruins. Dressed in red she said."

Daniel started, but Dominic held up his hand to stop him speaking.

"It was nothing though. George and Bob went up there and couldn't see a sign of anyone. One of the window frames had a bit of old curtain flapping around on it, so it must have been that. She'd cause a lot fewer problems if she just got on with her work."

Daniel tried to relax again. A curtain. It was nothing. He breathed slower and made himself focus again on the stew and the conversation. There was enough to worry about without jumping at ghosts. After the meal Dominic's mum and dad went through to a

134

back room. Dominic and Daniel stayed at the table.

"Traveller, tell me, what's it like – beyond the city?"

"What's it like?"

"I mean, is there anything? Are there safe places?"

"I don't think anywhere is safe Dominic. Nowhere there are people."

"But," Dominic paused. "Better than here?"

"Well, I feel safer away from this kind of place. Out in the woods, up to the north you can live a long time without seeing anyone – if you know how to find food, how to make shelter." But of course, by now everyone knew how to do that.

"I've never seen real forests. When I was small maybe – before the End. Since then, we've been here. Without Travellers, I wouldn't believe there was anything else. Most of the others don't. But Travellers have to come from somewhere." He stopped for a moment. "Of course, there might not be anything else. You might not be real."

Daniel looked at him and at himself. "I'm definitely real," he said but doubted it suddenly. Was this existence not like a fantasy?

"I think it's easier to believe there's nothing else sometimes," the boy said. "Or to pretend to believe it. You wanted to be alone."

"Yes I – you see a lot for a – for someone so young."

"I've always been able to. I don't know why."

"It must help you – your parents are proud of you, I think."

"It doesn't help me make friends. But yes, it helps the adults, what I see."

"And what do you see when you look at me?"

"You know – a Traveller."

"Which means?"

"I don't know – different."

"How?"

"I'm not supposed to say. It's a rule."

"Whose rule? Your parents'? Why?"

"Not theirs, not anyone's. I just know it. No, there's no point" – Daniel had grabbed hold of the boy's wrist. "I can't tell you Traveller, I can't."

Daniel relaxed his grip and drew his hand back, "I'm sorry, I'm ..."

"You can't pretend there's nobody else anymore. So now what you are means something."

"You have so much here."

"Except, we're eating through our stores. Very slowly, but year by year it's happening. There are always plans but with the Sects you're never sure what will happen. If they find a field or a cache, it's theirs. Of course, we always have someone on guard and usually they can divert their attention – it's risky but we've got hiding places everywhere – a few minutes' chase and they're away from the crops. And luckily, they don't search too much – they have their own system and produce enough food of their own. But when they get more settled, if their numbers go up –"

"Your parents don't see it?"

"There's still enough reasons not to take a risk. What if there were Sects everywhere? What if the conditions somewhere else weren't right for growing? What about the old people – and the little ones?"

"You can't be responsible for all of them. You have to survive."

"Alone?"

Yes, alone, thought Daniel. Moving, fighting, moving. But maybe he could help. Maybe it would make up for all the people he'd looked down on and avoided and hated. Maybe it would make up for – that other thing.

"It's not Sects everywhere, I've seen that much. And there's land, fields not so long out of cultivation. Fish, rabbits, all of that."

"But the flu?"

"No more, or less risk than here, I think."

Dominic nodded. "Thank you Traveller."

"Daniel. I'm Daniel. You never knew? About the outside?"

"You're the first I've spoken to like this – well, the first that's wanted to answer. Most are from round here – the city. They can't tell any more than we know already, or they keep it to themselves. As if it still mattered to them." He smiled sadly.

"Things don't just stop mattering." Daniel thought and said at once.

Dominic looked at him. "You're right, Traveller – Daniel. Family, friends – you can't just leave them to save yourself."

Daniel did not reply.

"But if there's somewhere to go, maybe we could all get there."

And there was somewhere, Daniel realised – that little cottage overlooking the plain. "There is a place, up beyond the plain – about three days walk – well, say a week for a group." Another thought occurred to him. "Perhaps I could ..."

Dominic caught the look in his eye. "That you want to is enough. But your path is not ours."

"It's alone."

"Yes. But tell me the way – the landmarks, the route – my parents will know it, or the others will, from before the End. If I can persuade them."

And Daniel told him: the cathedral, the industrial ruins, the waves of houses and shops, the pool and the heron, the telescope, the motorway, the path across the floods – all the way to Sylvia's door and those quiet woods – like tracing a path home. He finished his instructions faster than he wanted. There was nothing else to give. Dominic thanked him again, and then stood.

"You can sleep here Traveller." He motioned to a pallet of straw to one side of the room. "We'll be next door. At dawn, I'll show you the way out of the city."

Again, Dominic read the longing in Daniel's eyes. He must have seen it before in others. "You know you have somewhere to go Traveller. In the end, it will be worth the pain."

There could be no sign in this closed bunker to show that the sun was rising over the broken city above, but Dominic woke him some time later, placing a candle on the table and starting to clear the ash of the previous night's fire from the range. Once Daniel had dressed, the boy led him in silence back out into the city. The sky was a washed out pink and the air had a chill that would recede as the sun continued to climb. Along winding, indistinct paths through the rubble they walked, until they came to a wider road.

"I have to leave you here Traveller, but this is your way. You'll find the hills to the south if you keep going along here. But it's more than a day's walk."

Then Dominic echoed those first words of his mother the night before – "Remember us at your destination."

"I will," said Daniel, but his heart was empty. Had this been his last chance to form real bonds, more than the transient acquaintances of the road? He had to keep going. He had to follow the path. The boy looked at him with gentle eyes.

"Don't be sad to leave – we'll meet you again."

"Thank you," said Daniel. "And good luck to all of you." And the boy was gone, back into the greyness of broken walls, the emptiness of the past.

*

Daniel walked all day but, as the light began to seep away, the city still stretched out around him. He needed somewhere safe to rest. He was in an industrial area again. Elaborate ducts, vents, conduits, and conveyor belts linked collapsing sheds, loomed over by smoke-blackened chimneys. Older mills with lines of windows like empty eye sockets stared out at the roads in front of them, over areas of cleared ground that were now a tangle of buddleia, birch, and willowherb. He passed what had once been a pub, on a corner surrounded by wasteland, like a single dead tree left in the middle of a clear-felled forest. Once it must have stood shoulder to shoulder with the terraced houses that would have lined every street around here. A community that had been destroyed long before the End, pulled apart while the pulse of humanity was strong. Everyone had said 'that's the way of things' – he'd said it himself, talking to those undergrads at that party. A race. But a race to where?

He looked around. This was no place to sleep, but he had to stop; it was almost dark, and the moon would not rise for a few hours. Nearby, the door to a warehouse hung open, and he slipped inside, pulling the heavy metal door to behind him – the sound of it being pushed open would alert him to anyone following him in. Water dripped from splits in the corrugated roof, and the last faint glimmer of daylight filtered in through dirt-streaked skylights. He crossed the concrete floor to high, empty metal shelves. The lowest was raised far enough off the floor that it was dry. It was a deep shelf that must have held sheets of wood; a few stray squares of hardboard littered the floor close by. At the back of the shelf, the warehouse wall had corroded away. If he used boarding to fill that gap and to protect him at the front, this should be a relatively safe, if not pleasant, place to rest.

He followed his plan, feeding the board out through the gap in the wall so it rested outside it – it filled the hole but, if necessary, he could kick it away and slip out into the yard behind. The same

139

arrangement on the other side gave him two escape routes and would conceal him. The board on the inside was low enough to leave a gap between its top and the shelf above, giving him a view of the shed without exposing him. He settled as best he could, eating the last of his fish before darkness enfolded the building completely.

Sometime in the middle of the night he woke from fitful sleep. His knapsack was digging into his back, but that was not what had disturbed him. Water still dripped onto the concrete with an uneven patter. Through the slit-window between board and shelf the warehouse was blue grey with the light of the waning moon. What woke him had been a scraping sound of metal on concrete. Unless he had imagined the sound, someone had pushed open the warehouse door. But now there was silence. He began to think that his paranoia had created the sound in his dreams. Gradually he began to relax. Even if the noise had been real, it could have been a fox or badger knocking against something as it foraged. But then he heard the slow, echoing sound of footsteps. Somebody was walking across the concrete floor towards the shelves. He thought of what Dominic's dad had said. Someone in red, watching. Or hunting.

He sensed the derelict city rolling endlessly away in all directions. None of its decaying buildings, shattered streets, overgrown parks, held anything that could help him, except for Dominic and his little community, and that might as well be a hundred miles away. He clasped his bag and braced his foot against the boarding covering the outer wall. He didn't move – whoever it was surely had no way to know he was there. The steps were close now – ten metres, five, three – one of the boards on the warehouse floor was kicked aside with a crack that echoed around the empty amphitheatre. Those boards were right in front of the shelving. Who is it that comes? The grey light through the gap between board and shelf was cut off by a shadow. He saw a dark coloured coat. He could hear someone breathing, as he held his own breath. The second seemed to last an hour, until he thought that whoever it was must turn away. There was a rustle of clothes – were they looking round? Had they given up? Then, very close, familiar eyes stared straight into his,

"Hello Mr Fox," whispered Harry.

If you should see him again, you must run.

Harry wrenched back the board covering the inner side of the shelf, as Daniel kicked away the outer one. The hunter's hand reached in at him, but he was already rolling out, dropping onto the concrete apron of the yard. The fall knocked the breath out of him for a second, and he struggled to his feet, gasping for air. Then he did run, not waiting to see Harry clamber out into the moonlight behind him. The yard was enclosed, and in the dark he could not make out the doorways and windows that must have been set into the walls that surrounded it. But the moon lit a narrow ramp, the bed of a chute or conveyor-belt that ran up the outside of the factory wall. It was wide enough for a person, and not too steep. There didn't seem to be any other option. He pulled himself up onto it. A metallic groan, a screech from rusted fastenings, but the ramp held firm. He ran upwards, as fast as he dared given the unguarded drop that grew to his left as he climbed.

The city was jagged and black under the moonlight – no torch or lamp illuminated the sprawl. Flood water gleamed between flats and offices. The air was cold, the ramp freezing under his feet, reverberating and creaking with every heavy step he took. Suddenly, he felt the whole structure sink a few inches, and there was a sound of tearing metal. Harry had climbed up below him. Still his precarious path held, and he reached the top. The channel disappeared into the black maw of some kind of processing machine. There was pipe-work stretching above the ramp between this warehouse and the next building and he swung himself up onto it. From there he hauled himself across onto the flat roof. He began to make his way along the edge, precarious on the steel frame of the building, between the drop and panelling buckled and twisted with age. Now Harry was on the beam too. His laughter rang out in the night air

"Where *are* you going, Mr Fox?"

141

And suddenly, he had nowhere to go. In front of him a section of the beam on which he walked had fallen away, and there was a gaping hole in the building where the wall and part of the roof had collapsed completely. He began to edge round it, trusting his weight to thin, corroded metal that gave alarmingly as he crawled across it. By necessity he was slowed, and Harry was close – two or three metres behind at most. He reached a line of bolts, indicating another beam underlying the roofing sheets – relative safety. But behind him, Harry stood up straight. A strange compulsion made Daniel turn to look at him. Both were still, the sound of ragged breathing loud, tortured creaks from the metal sheets below them.

"What's the point in this?" Daniel shouted. "Why do you want me dead? I've done nothing to you!"

"Dead?" Harry laughed. "Very funny, Traveller. Yes," he continued, all the time shuffling imperceptibly forwards. "I'm going to kill you – you're in an action movie. Just run and save the day – you'll be fine."

"What the hell are you talking about?"

And now Daniel looked into his eyes. Whether by a trick of the moonlight or of his exhausted state, they seemed entirely black. But the blackness was not a colour. It was an absence of – anything. And he could not tear himself away from their stare.

Harry's voice was quiet now. "How can you understand what I want, if you don't know who I am?"

Daniel knew now why Sylvia had told him to run. He drew his machete. The figure that was once Harry Linton just strode forward. Perhaps three steps separated them. But on the second, the sheeting beneath its feet disintegrated. It was pitched forward. Daniel saw the flesh of its hand torn open as it reached back up in its fall, catching only a rusted edge of metal. There was a silence that lasted a heartbeat, and then a thud below. Straining his eyes, he could see the dark shape of the body, with blackness spreading out onto the concrete around it.

*

It took Daniel a long time to get down off the roof, working his way gingerly along the metal beams. He was forced to move with methodical caution, with that black shape below him in the dark. Under the clear sky, it was bitterly cold. A thin breeze blew down from the north and chilled him to the bone. His hands were numb from feeling his way over the metal panels, frightened to stand lest he ended up sharing the fate of the hunter. It seemed like an eternity before he got to the chute and edged his way down to the ground, and as he reached it, he saw that the features of the yard and the surrounding buildings were now picked out by the spreading light of dawn.

Ducking back through the hole in the warehouse wall, he hurried across the open space within. He did not look left, into the gloom, and wrenched the door of the shed closed behind him. Then he ran – out between plots of wasteland on a narrow feeder road, along a wider street with dead traffic lights and roundabouts fountaining with unmanaged foliage. A wave of estates broke around him, rows of houses, then older terraces, a shopping centre. Finally, he stopped, leaning against the wall of a derelict shop and struggling for breath.

That's far enough.

He pushed down his fear. He had to rest, at least for a couple of hours. He walked slowly along the street, still gathering his breath. An alley led off the road, cutting between the yards of two rows of terraced houses. He followed it over cobbles shining and wet with the recent rain. About fifty metres along a van was parked. One of the back doors had been forced, and now it was rusted open. The windscreen was also smashed. So, it had two exits. It was dry, and he would be hidden inside. He could lie behind the closed door, and the driver's seat would cover him at the front. He crawled in, wrapped himself in his blanket. For a long time he lay there, staring

143

at the rusted roof, until fatigue overcame his anxiety.

Awaking with a start a few hours later he was immediately alert. But the noise that had dragged him back to consciousness was just the patter of rain on the roof of the van. It was late morning, judging from the angle of the watery sunlight shining through the broken windscreen. Time to move – again. Had he not been better off in the mountains? At least there he hadn't lived in fear, at least he hadn't been hunted. There, nature supported him; here it disintegrated the remains of the civilisation that had nurtured him. But the thought of turning back was resisted by something deep within him, whatever arguments he raised against it. Once more, he began to walk – the city must peter out soon.

After a couple of hours, he at last came to the outskirts, where the life of the countryside met the decay of human structure – one still, the other in constant flux. Trees were in a struggle against the concrete, over the years inserting their roots into foundations and disintegrated them, thrusting branches through walls with irresistible slow-motion punches. And beyond that front line, fields reclaimed by the forest that was once more a place of fairy tale menace and fairy tale hope. He moved forward eagerly. A shower of rain that had followed the sun up over the horizon moved on, and the morning was quiet – he heard none of the cries and shouts that had disturbed his walk through the city. Grateful to be back in a natural landscape, he traversed the young woodlands that filled the once-open fields, then climbed gently through an older, denser forest in the gentle afternoon light. Clouds were gathering to the north.

He wanted to put at least one ridge between himself and the city behind him. Between himself and Harry. The landscape became more open as he walked, lost in his thoughts. Gorse and mountain ash peppered the hillside; this would have been a common in the old days. The short-cropped grass was still maintained by stocky feral ponies which poached the ground along the pathways through the stands of furze. A skylark rose above him with its trilling call, and a flock of linnets, brown and red, swirled away over the scrub. But further out on the common something was different. There were no larks now, and even the ponies seemed to have melted away. Black clouds were massing above. He saw a silhouette; a post and a beam and something else. It was incongruous, it should not have been. A shadow from an earlier age.

A crow was busy picking at – something. He strained to see in the gloom, hoping it wasn't what he thought. But as he came closer there was no doubt. A corpse dangled from the beam, and it was the flesh on its face that the crow was devouring. Catching sight of him the bird started up, flapping into the sky to be lost against the clouds. The scene made no sense. Daniel had seen no sign of people since he had left Dominic. He was miles from the city, and yet this body was still fresh enough to give the crows a meal. He shivered.

Now he was on one of the roads that met at the gibbet, and he was aware of a slow, regular creaking as the body swung patiently in the gusting wind. He was drawn to it, just as he had been held by the hunter's eyes on the rooftop. He wanted to turn and run but found he could not. He reached the crossroads and the figure on the frame filled his vision. Everything else was dark and the only sound was that gentle creaking. He felt a wave of resentment against the family that had forced him to carry on alone, rather than share their hospitality. The same rejection he had faced in his old life. A rejection that met him time and again, that forced him on from everything he had ever cared for. In his mind's eye the broken face of the old thief grinned at him and inside he felt again the adrenalin kick of violence, the joy of releasing that anger. The freedom of it.

Now the figure ahead was completely black. It was more than a silhouette – an effect of the light – it was darkness, a hole in the light. It was the emptiness he had faced up on the warehouse roof. There was no way except into that hole. Step by step he drew closer, and the sound of the wind, the fading daylight, the grass and the gorse disintegrated and slipped from his senses. The horror was around him, over him, and he felt an icy cold. One more step –

But as he moved forward, the stillness was broken by a gentle breeze. A warm breath on his cheek, a comforting touch, full where

145

the blackness was empty. Blown by that breeze, a sprig of fennel, blue-green in the dark, tumbled lightly across the ground in front of him. Torn from the spell, he watched it as it drifted onto the road that led west. He was not alone. He turned away from the corpse, from the vortex. But as he did so a hand reached out to clutch him, dragging him back. The arm of its coat was red, and the soft, rotting legs of the corpse wore blood-smattered jodhpurs. The body jerked as it pulled him into its embrace, its broken skull, writhing with maggots, leered down. The stench of death filled his nostrils. With a violent wrench he ripped himself free of those mangled hands, pushing the thing away from him, the figure still twitching like a puppet. An inhuman cry rent the air. Then he ran, towards the west, towards the shafts of sunlight that fanned down onto the hills from between the glowering clouds. Behind him, if he had looked, he would have seen that there was no gibbet on the hill, only the four roads and the gorse and the sky.

Chapter 12

Over the next few days, he walked through a landscape of rolling hills, wide valleys, streams, and rivers that wound through woods and across the softening pattern of the abandoned landscape. Sometimes the hills were high enough to be topped by heath and moorland, where shards of stone were scattered amongst bilberry and heather, and grouse chuckled to each other and flew up at his approach. These wide, lofty uplands, gentler than their northern counterparts, offered vistas of trees and fields, rural scenes that from a distance might still have been managed by thriving human communities. Only walking through these old pastures and arable plots did the regenerating clusters of birch and ash, the hedges exploding up and out from their narrow confines, show how nature was reasserting its authority. These places had never seen cities or towns, and just as modernity had only touched them lightly, so the changes now were subtle — nature did not have to punch her way out from under concrete here.

He was changing too, as he watched that gentle evolution at work around him. The laws of physics, the cellular structures of living things, their evolutionary lineages, must still exist. But now things were just what they were. The trees were shelter, the sun warmth and light, the streams and plants food and drink, and all these things were much more too. He felt like a participant, not a consumer. These things were not just for him. He prayed — not as he had in those first days after he left Carl, prayers of shame and fear, but meditations, thanks. Despite that, he was not completely settled. Once, as he gathered berries in an open forest where mist lay around the trees, he saw a woman, naked, walking some way off. He stared at her, at her movement as she walked through long, dewy grass that brushed her thighs and her fingers. Was it the light through the trees that gave her skin that emerald glow? She looked up at him and smiled and he started to move towards her. And she was gone. Sadness. Woman.

A test? A temptation?

He had a sense of something coming. There was still something to be balanced.

Three days later and after a long day's walk, his path took him along an open, sloping hillside. The warmth of the season rose up from the land, the fresh, new grass under his feet was like balm, blossom smothered the cherry and crab apple trees. There were more flowers on the hawthorns lining the old field boundaries in the valley below, like snow on the green. He strode along the ridge, no longer frightened of being seen. It was the gloaming, and the gentleness of the light made the landscape seem benevolent, nurturing.

He looked down at the saddle between the hill on which he stood and the next. Trees grouped in the shadows of the night as the sun set, they flowed in dark green waves over the far summit. On the grazed turf, two figures stood; a tall, broad man with a green-wood staff, and a woman. The light was fading and he couldn't make out their features from so far away. He scrambled down the steep escarpment, watching his step over loose stones. When he reached the saddle, there was only the man, gazing upwards. Following his eyes, Daniel looked up into the darkness of the sky and, for a second, he was sure he saw, between the clouds, a figure with a black, streaming blanket wrapped round her as she climbed to the stars.

"Is that...?"

The man turned. There were leaves in his hair where it fell around a cap of strange bark. His solid, jovial face was as brown as a nut, and he was bearded.

"Do not worry after her; she's gone to brush cobwebs down from the sky, but she'll be back with us by and by – "

The man looked out over the darkening plain, overgrown fields in the dying light seeming for a moment to return to a previous state, when their backs were clean yellow after the harvest. Were

148

there lights down there? Workers trailing back at the end of the day, scythes over their shoulders, dust and sweat mixing on their brows?

"They have chased the spirit of the corn to the centre of the field, their blades catching the sun, the taste of ale on their lips. They take the final stem and cut it and bind it into a doll and carry it aloft with the spirit intact and set it to watch over them 'til the next harvest comes around; around and around until they are gone and others take their place, until the others have forgotten them, until there are no others."

Daniel followed the man's gaze over that shifting plain of light and dark, past and present. "You're sad that it's gone?"

"Gone?" The man laughed "All is there together, at one at the same time as it is divided."

The man looked away from the plain and the fields, and the illusion, if there had been one, was replaced by shadow as the sun finally gave way to the night. His gaze rested on Daniel now. Although his face was kind, it had a dark aspect. Daniel sensed a threat in the disconcerting depth of those eyes.

"Are you one who cuts the bark from the live wood, who tears the limbs of trees for fire?"

He felt compelled to give a truthful answer – "I suppose I've done that, one way or another. But I want to put it right." And he did want to. He didn't want to be alone anymore. The large man's eyes softened.

"Good. You may pass through this bower of mine, not because of your words – for words are empty sounds – but because of what is in your heart. And the fruits of the land will be shown to you and its ways will be open to you. For surely you are no more of that kind."

Daniel smelt soil, wood, vegetation, the smell of the forest after rain. And the man laughed deeply and threw back his head, and from his mouth burst forth foliage and stems that thickened to branches and his arms by his sides lengthened and his fingers were

149

buried in the soil. His limbs widened and his skin hardened to ridged grey bark and before Daniel there was an ancient oak with a wide, solid bole and spreading branches, heavy with the green, early buds of acorns. And when he reached out and touched the bark, he thought he heard a faint echo of laughter mixing with the soughing of the wind in the boughs.

Somehow, he found he was comforted by what should have been disturbing. What would have been incredible to him before now seemed to fit seamlessly into this world of dreams. Transformation was no surprise. No more than his own transformation.

That evening he slept deeply in a mossy hollow, surrounded by oak trees and protected by holly and the silver-brown stems of old hazel coppice. Waking at dawn, he watched the shuffling progress of a badger following a path through the hollow, snuffling at the ground for last season's nuts, for grubs and worms and the scent of rabbits or hedgehogs. Its beady, short-sighted eyes did not spot Daniel, motionless on his bed of moss, and a slight breeze took his scent from the animal. It was a heavy old male, barrelling along the path traced by it, and others in its sett, over many seasons of foraging. The animal's breath mingled with the mist, the fur on his striped head and grey back glinted with droplets of dew; he was so close that Daniel could hear his footfalls.

All the next day he walked, almost bounding, through the dappled light of the forest. His eyes picked out every leaf, every pale and delicate flower. There was something else too, at the corner of his eye sometimes when he stopped to rest or forage; movement, flowing, sensuous, feminine. But as the afternoon shadows grew long his path took him downhill, and his mood changed. The sense of joy and yearning receded. The birds were silent. He came to a clearing and stopped abruptly. A small fire was burning there, unattended. By it was a backpack, and a blanket was laid out. Immediately he turned to get away, but he was too slow. A man stepped out from behind a tree, with a rifle trained on him.

"Don't move."

Daniel eyed him. He was tall, his height accentuated by a long black, mud-stained coat. From a narrow, gaunt face red-rimmed eyes stared intensely, his hair tucked roughly back in a dark, makeshift ponytail.

"I'm just passing through – I'm no threat."

"No threat?" The man laughed. "Everyone is a threat." He took a pace forwards, away from the tree, looking over Daniel's shoulder towards the fire. "Tell me. Are you a God-fearing man?"

Without pause Daniel confessed. "I am."

"OK," the man nodded. "Easy to say, but I wonder. 'In you, lord my God I put my trust, I trust in you; do not let me be put to shame'."

"Psalm 25." Good teaching by his parents, back in those innocent days. Slowly, the man lowered his rifle.

"I'm glad." His gladness was unsmiling. "I had a feeling about you, when I was watching you walking up there, through the woods. I thought, this is maybe one that can pass the test."

"Test?"

The man ignored the question. "Come, brother, will you break bread with me?"

Daniel nodded. He knew the type, although in his parents' prayer meetings they hadn't been so well-armed. At a gesture from him, Daniel walked into the clearing and sat down with him by the fire.

"I am Saul. What's your name, friend?"

"Daniel – although everyone calls me Traveller now."

"You as well?" The man asked. Daniel felt an emptiness in the pit of his stomach. "Well, the lord brings humility. I'd imagined there was a special significance to that name – for me I mean. But maybe they just call everyone that."

"Yes."

151

Saul reached over to his pack and brought out some roots and leaves, some salted meat.

"I don't want to take your food – I haven't foraged today – I don't have anything."

"You have your story, and you have your time." Saul held out some of the food. "Don't be concerned – I'm free of disease."

Daniel took what was offered, and they ate. But he was not sure he wanted this companion, and not sure how he could get away from him – the rifle was close to Saul's side.

"I'm going back," said Saul suddenly.

"Back where?"

"To where I came from in the first place – down in the city. There's work to do there."

"Work?"

"The Lord's work."

So long as he wasn't expected to follow, that was fine.

"And you?"

"I've come a long way – from the north, through the city." Daniel sensed, rather than saw an imperceptible shift in Saul's position, a tensing that brought him and the gun closer.

"Why do you keep moving?" Saul fixed him again with those intense eyes.

"I don't know. I feel I should."

Saul's hand was on the rifle now. "You follow that feeling?"

"I think it's God's will for me." That seemed to be a good answer because, although Saul carried on staring at him, he brought his hand away from the gun again.

"I see. You're on the wide path by mistake, without realising. Then there is a chance for you. Thank God for this opportunity to share. Listen to what I have to tell you."

Daniel glanced at the darkening sky.

"Don't worry about finding somewhere – you can sleep here tonight. No harm will come to us – we were meant to meet, it seems."

It also seemed that that was an offer it would be unwise to refuse. "OK. What do you want to tell me?"

Saul laughed. "Funny isn't it? the pattern of things now – since the End. Every conversation has the same pattern – a challenge, a confrontation, an exchange and a decision."

"A decision?"

"About who should live. Not necessarily our own decision, of course – sometimes the decision of circumstance or chance. But God's decision, by whatever means."

Daniel kept quiet and waited. Saul stared into the fire for a while and when he spoke his voice was not much more than a whisper.

"At the End – right at the end – I was in a church. There were about sixty people there I suppose. We had food and water and shelter." He paused. "It's hard to describe – we were – we were a family. Different from the family I'd had before," he added. "Loyal. To be trusted."

What lay behind his tone when he said that? A silent house with half the things gone? A hand-written letter on the kitchen table?

"I thought we might get through it all, holed up there. We were all healthy, and the building was modest, out of the way – nothing to attract attention. But of course, someone did pay attention. Maybe they saw a light in a window when someone was careless with the blinds, or maybe they heard something. Whatever. They broke down the door and started shooting."

"What did they want?"

"Want? How can you ask that? You must have been through it

153

too? It wasn't rational, it wasn't thought out. They didn't *want* anything, except to kill. To rape. In the aisles of a church."

"Oh."

"Not much to be said is there? Once you've seen that. Not much mercy there is there?"

"How did you…?"

"I don't know. I must have blacked out. I was there, watching them as they …" He broke off for a moment. "I was there. And then I was outside, and it was getting light, and no-one was left."

"I'm – sorry."

"I had my bag with me, somehow, and I had my bible." He pulled a battered King James' bible from his bag, it's hard back cover closed over a wad of pages that was not thick enough to fill it.

"What happened to it?"

"The pages you mean? Ha, well. I had to revise it. Once I'd worked things out."

"Revise it?" Into Daniel's mind came the image of a vertical black line on a smudged white canvas.

"You have to understand what the End was." Saul sighed and poked at the fire, sending flurries of golden embers spiralling skywards. "It was a test – He'd given us the Commandments, He'd sent His son. But we rejected it all. The End was the consequence."

"But," Daniel glanced at the bible again. "Why?"

"A difficult one isn't it – 'Why?'. The End was us returning to the beasts, rejecting even our humanity. Rejecting God's image. 'Love Thy Neighbour'. Ha! You have to be human for that message to apply. And if you're not, then the New Testament isn't for you. It's not for beasts. The rule book for them is the old rule book."

He picked up the bible, turned to an obviously well-used page – the book falling open on it almost by itself – and read quietly:

154

"I will demand an accounting for the life of another human being – whoever sheds human blood, by humans shall their blood be shed."

Daniel shivered, close as he was to the warmth of the fire.

"The book of Genesis. God's covenant with Noah. The symmetry is inescapable. If we are still human, if we are still in God's image, then the instruction is clear. We must settle the accounts. Until there is Balance."

"But, weren't people desperate? I mean, you can't blame all of them ..."

"People were tested," corrected Saul. "If they failed in that test, they have to face the consequence. Just like we did when they had the power. Listen, do you think it was an accident that I was saved? That my Bible was saved? That this answer came to me?"

"You were lucky to get away. Very lucky."

"Luck! It was more than luck. He needed a Judge, and he chose me."

"So you –?"

"I Judge. No," he corrected himself. "The Book judges – and I pass sentence."

"Oh." Daniel had seen that kind of sentence passed.

"How many people?"

"How many sinners, you mean? I don't keep count."

"And how many are innocent?"

He shook his head. "There's no innocence left. But with you, Daniel, I hold out hope. I'm getting tired, and my work is getting harder." He looked up from the fire and stared at Daniel. "You would come with me?"

"Of – Of course, if you need me."

155

"Then," Saul straightened his back and his tone lightened. "It's time for us to sleep. Tomorrow I will Judge you and, God willing we'll go on together."

Daniel felt the space around them, rolling, empty miles of woodland, and himself separated from it. They settled down, either side of the dying fire.

"And Daniel – I sleep lightly. Don't imagine you can slip away. You would be judging yourself."

Daniel lay awake, thinking. There was no point trying to slip off in the night – if Saul woke up, he would shoot him, and if not, he would follow him.

What then – stay here and wait to be butchered?

True, it might only be a matter of time. With someone like that. He couldn't run and he couldn't stay. He breathed slower, steadying his thoughts. OK. They weren't the only options. Saul seemed to have some idea that he might be on his side. That meant he might be persuaded to let him go. If the argument fitted with his version of faith. Then, it would have to be God – the reason. God wanted their paths to go in different directions. That might work.

And the judgement?

The judgement would be OK – Saul needed him – or thought he did.

Unless he leaves it to chance – what page will the book fall open at, that kind of thing. But –

But it can't be that random, if he's killed them all. Which means that he does control it. Or he interprets things to make them fit what he wants. Above, stars dusted the sky, crowding it with light. They drew him out and away and somehow, he slept.

And then it was dawn, as if no time had passed. With his eyes still closed he tensed, remembering where he was, and who he was with. But when he opened them and sat up, he was alone by the ashes of the fire. Saul's knapsack was there, his blanket. Not his gun though. Was this a chance?

No, remember. He has to let you go, otherwise –

As his senses focussed, Daniel heard a sound like an irregular drumbeat, sporadic and muffled by distance. It was the sound of an axe against wood, but the rhythm was disjointed, uneven. Desperate. And he felt a strange thing – he felt pain, washing over him, surging through the forest. Struggling to his feet he took his knapsack and blanket and started to jog towards the sound, compelled by the sensation that, as it rose inside him, was fear as well as pain. The wood sloped downwards, fog weaved around the trunks of the trees. After about two hundred metres he emerged from a hem of hazel and wych elm. There was a meadow deep with flowers and grasses, glittering with dew under the rising sun. Beside this sparkling bowl, in amongst an outlying spur of ash trees, was Saul. He was swinging a felling axe, weary but intent. Where had he found it? A little way from him lay one tree, already felled, its upturned leaves pale, the stump from which it had been hewn protruding brokenly from the ground. As Daniel moved towards him, the blade of the axe made the final incision into the tree Saul was hacking at, and it crashed down across the other. Exhausted though he clearly was, he staggered towards the next.

"Stop!" Daniel ran, leaping over the fallen trunks. Saul ignored him. The axe swung back once more, but now Daniel was close enough to grab it. Unbalanced, Saul fell, and whatever determination had driven him, Daniel's intervention gave fatigue a chance to overwhelm it. Suddenly Saul was weeping, shaking. Where was his gun? He didn't have it near him at any rate. If he could find that –

"What the hell were you doing?"

Saul raised himself up against the trunk of the tree he had been about to attack. "Cleansing this," Saul waved his arms. "This place."

"Cleansing it?"

"Yes," his voice cracked. "I saw her when I woke, out in the forest. Tempting me."

Daniel said nothing. He knew who Saul meant.

"I followed her here. This is her place. And I found this." He pointed to the axe. "Down there, by the wall. The judgement was made for me."

"Yes."

"Then help me. I can't do any more. But it's not enough. I can still feel her."

"I'm sorry, Saul. This isn't right."

Saul's expression hardened – "Then get away from me." But then he froze, staring beyond Daniel as if he had forgotten he existed. Daniel turned, angry at himself for dropping his guard. By him stood the Green Man – the man who was a tree. There was no echo of laughter about him now.

"You waste your time on this one. The seed within him has starved and died."

Daniel looked at Saul with sudden pity. "He's not well –"

But the Green Man never took his eyes from Saul. "He is dead already. It is part of the order."

He moved to stand over Saul, and his bulk hid him from view. And when he moved again there was nothing where he had been. Then the Green man walked to the two tree stumps, and at each he paused and tapped the surface with his green-wood staff. Daniel saw seedlings emerge where the staff had touched. They grew and sprouted, erupting upwards in a burst of life until they stood as mature trees again, settling as if they had been there for decades. A robin, sitting on those fallen limbs that still covered the ground, sang loudly. And the Green Man was gone, and Daniel was alone.

Chapter 13

The next night was a cold one. Making camp Daniel lit a fire, keeping it going after he had eaten to provide warmth under clear, star speckled skies. He slept poorly, in his mind the fear in Saul's eyes, the Green Man standing over him. The space where he had been.

"He is dead already"

The next day the weather remained fair, and he walked quickly, lost in his thoughts. For several miles he followed a clear, fast-running stream, in the shade of alder and crack willow, the yellow flowers of creeping buttercup at his feet and the occasional iridescent blue of a kingfisher flashing past, low to the water. Then the valley curved away to the north, and he began to ascend, keeping his way to the south west. At the summit of a low hill he came to a glade, its edges blurred by foliage, the light on the long grass and wildflowers dappled and warm. It was only mid-afternoon but his lack of sleep the night before impelled him to rest. He took off his knapsack and lay down in the sun among the grass and the flowers. Bumblebees stooped at the blooms to dip their tongues into the nectar hidden amongst the delicate petals, and a warbler sang a melody that rose and fell and swirled, weaving the air around him. Time drifted and eventually he slept.

The Golden Man was sitting beneath a tree and his mind was at rest. Cross-legged he meditated, and the chasing particles of light in his head extended into waves and joined and what was separate was one and all potentialities were recognised and existed at once. The light radiated from him – and from the trees, the grass, the animals and birds, the same light emanated and joined, and he saw each unreduced, and he did not allow his gaze to disintegrate their unity and they were freed of that constraint and his senses encompassed the Golden Glade.

And then Daniel's dream changed. He was lying on the grass and his arms were by his sides, palms down, his back, his legs, his head against the ground. He felt the pulse of the sap, reached down green wet channels that turned to white and then were enclosed in darkness, narrowing, twisting and turning until they were one with the sweet, damp, black earth. He felt around blindly with the pink fleshy body of an earthworm, bristles pushing him through the soil that he sensed and understood, shaped with his movement, feeding on it, excreting it. There was the vibration of the rock below, the core beneath it, capillaries of molten lava deep down, inside but alone. Up now, back up through dark and white and green to chewing jaw and hot warmth of stomach and in arteries of thick blood beneath soft fur, over bone, looking out of dark shining eyes, smelling through wet black nose, feeling grass crushed by rounded teeth, a relaxed satisfaction of thought, an underlying and never ceasing alertness. And at the same time without losing the sensation of any of these, he was within the strong feathered breast of a bird, leaves, branches, grass below, air rushing, sinews stretching and relaxing, eyes cast around. He was burrowing with sharp, hard claws, scraping out dark rounded corridors and within them warm dry hay, wriggling pink young suckling blindly at a heavy body, taking in creamy, hot milk, bellies expanding. He swooped with the night, fine, elastic warm wings flickering, sound spurting out between needle-teeth, feeling and judging the returning waves, turning acrobatically in response, picking out the moon-lured moth, grey and cool. He coiled and sprang with the fleas from regular-heaving harbours of fine-haired waves, without repulsion burrowing with tiny larvae within the flesh of a caterpillar, released and unfurled with the flower from its encasing emerald bud, drinking deep the nectar.

Gently he woke, and in that moment between sleeping and waking he was sure he felt the touch of lips on his lips, the brush of long hair against his cheek, the surge of a woman's body against his – and his eyes opened, and he was lying in the glade. He was alone but, straight away, he had the sense of being watched, and although that feeling lacked the menace it should have held, it drew him to

160

his feet. A woman stood only a foot or two from him, gazing at him with wide, hazel eyes. It was the woman he had seen before. She was slender, her emerald dress shimmering and dancing with the sunlight through the leaves. The smooth curves of her body were defined by its close-fitting, ephemeral material, which traced her form almost like a skin waiting to be cast off. All this he took in, but most striking was the colour of her real skin; unlined, unblemished it was tinted with the green of hart's tongue ferns. Round her face her hair flowed, long and dark brown, the colour of earth or seasoned wood, shining like mahogany over her shoulders and to her waist.

She stepped towards him with a lithe, flowing movement that brought her close in a second, and those hazel eyes beckoned. He took a step forward, and they were almost touching. Holding his gaze, she raised her arms and lifted her hair back from her face, so it flowed in a wave down her back and revealed the shape of her neck, her delicate ears. Still she said nothing, and instinctively he put his hands up onto her shoulders and with gentle firmness began to slip the soft dress from her. She made no move away as the emerald shimmer of material slid from her breasts. Instead, she reached out and pulled open his shirt and he drew her close. They fell to the ground together and he kissed her, her mouth yielding, her legs spread on the warm grass. As her tongue slid against his he thought he felt at its tip a groove, almost a fork. But the idea that crossed his mind only made his desire stronger.

To him, it seemed she was every woman he had loved, or lusted after; every break-up, every fun, risky one-night stand. And afterwards he felt a sense of release from a yearning so deep he had ceased to notice that he experienced it. He felt free. She lay beside him, and they watched white clouds that began already to turn peach with coming evening, framed by buttercups, clover and the swaying heads of foxtail and yellow-rattle. He was about to speak, but she must have sensed it, put her elegant, soft hand to his mouth and answered him in thoughts that entered his mind without words.

"You wonder who I am – my tongue." She laughed, out loud, and the sound had the quality of the warbler's song that had

161

accompanied his earlier rest. "It didn't stop you though? That thought?"

As she spoke, the story of Adam and Eve, and the snake, arose in his mind.

"A poor representation, I always felt." She smiled.

He saw then – he'd been tempted, and he'd given in. Without even fighting it. The woman just gazed at him.

"It's a struggle, isn't it – to make it all fit together?"

"What will happen to me?"

"What *is* happening to you, you mean? Why don't you just embrace it, open yourself to it?"

"But if you're –?"

"And if I am? Did the story get it right? Or was there another reason for it?"

"I shouldn't."

"I thought you dropped 'shouldn't' a long time ago."

"How could you know that?"

"If this is a test, you have to choose."

He thought of Saul and his hatred, the men at the cathedral. Being trapped. Not seeing. He thought of the hunter and the snake and this woman. But no, those didn't fit together. They jarred. Of all those things what aligned? The Judge, the men who stoned the woman and the Hunter – they fitted. And on the other side? The snake and the woman. Knowingness against Nature. He chose.

"I'm glad," she said. "I like you."

What had he done?

"Who are you?"

"I am a spirit – the spirit of this place."

"A spirit? But we – "

She watched him with those rich brown eyes, and they were still dark with pleasure. "For a Traveller, things are different – it's the way of things." And she seemed then to project a sense of age and experience and an encompassing compassion that was almost overwhelming. He wondered – why different for a Traveller, why different for me? But as if he had turned away from her and she had taken his face in her hands and turned it tenderly back to hers, she drew his thoughts away from that line of reasoning.

"There is no point in the journey if you learn everything before you reach its end. Don't you want to know who I am? You only know what I am not."

"Are you like the tree-man, on the ridge?"

She laughed. "He is an ancient force, a guardian – perhaps. He isn't like me – he just IS. He has his own rules."

He thought, then, of the woman flying off to sweep cobwebs from the sky, and this brought the lightest laugh yet –

"She is no cleaning woman – it's just a saying he has for her flights – he has a poetic turn of phrase. She is human, a guardian of a different kind, and the freedom of the skies comes with her knowledge of herbs and roots; it is a gift, in return for her labours – a pleasure, not a chore."

"A witch?"

"Yes, you would call her that, as you would call me a devil." Again, she smiled, and he blushed. "But this story is being told the wrong way around. Quiet your mind and listen."

He watched the darkening sky and freed himself of other thoughts, and it was easy to do in this glade, with this girl of twenty and a thousand years. He turned to her, his mind open. In her eyes he found opening out again what he had dreamt; he saw the spiral darkness view of the bat, felt the outstretched growing fingers of branches and the slow explosion of buds, watched the grain of decaying wood in its infinite detail as he stepped lightly over its contours as a spider, dipped his head with the breeze like the buttercups, and lay at their heart as an insect, devouring nectar. All of it as one would feel the heartbeat of a lover, the close pulse of life. He felt her body extended and encompassing the landscape around her, unconfined, her fate intertwined in its fate, her care its cares, its disparate and fractured knowledge finding synthesis in her spirit, her form. A guardian and an inseparable part, the manifestation of its united consciousness, ever-changing but constant, and the closeness was the gift of togetherness with that natural whole that escapes every man.

He found himself among the trees of an ancient, open woodland and somehow he could sense it stretching away, feel without seeing the veteran trees, wide, squat and twisted, dotted between their younger brothers and sisters or clustered in groups eternally intertwined, saplings at the edges of grassy deer-grazed clearings emerging from the safe nursery of thorns and holly, a whole landscape and, before him a lithe, spiralling form of forest colours that was sensuous and aged, joyful and melancholic, naïve and experienced all at once, whose streamers of colour flowed from every living thing. And for a moment he followed those streamers out across the trees and the pasture, heath and streams to a limit, perhaps half a mile from the centre, and beyond that the fading fine tips of those streamers interweaved with those of similar spirits which themselves stretched from their own centres. He watched a lean, dark-skinned boar trot across the border, and it carried with it some of the light and colour from one realm to the next and the new place took in what it carried. And then his view was drawn back from that limit to the first place he had seen.

Now there was another figure in that place, a middle-aged woman, neatly but poorly dressed, collecting flowers and herbs. A sadness that was his own welled up for a moment. The swirling form he noticed was orientated towards her, its light on her and around her and he sensed – friendship.

But as he studied the form that danced before him more closely it filled his mind and stirred desire within him, that desire he had felt when the girl had stepped close to him in the glade, and suddenly the form was that of the girl at the same time as it was a swirl of colour. His mind drank her in, and his imagination raced once more, and he saw in the shadow of the trees a man watching the woman gathering herbs and the naked girl who stood by her. And then he saw the neatly but poorly dressed woman in a town square filled with people and the man was at the front of the crowd and she was swinging from a rope.

Daniel found he was sobbing, his tears soaked up by the long dark hair of the girl as she held him close.

"I'm sorry," he whispered, pulling back.

"Don't be sorry for your tears – they are what will save you." She gazed at Venus hanging between the velvet dark of night and the red satin of the sun's cloak. Daniel felt, again, the yearning that came on calm, summer evenings, listening to bird song in deep woodland, seeing stems of grass shake with the hidden progress of a vole or a mouse, hearing the call of an owl amid the gloaming, and smelling the scent of earth and of nature – that subtle edge that defines coming autumn, that feeling that had overtaken him on so many occasions. That yearning that had taken him into the woods all those years ago. A sweet melancholy that the moment of enjoyment was fleeting and incomplete, that he was a visitor, separated from the life he observed. Separated by imagination, an endless pool of possibilities that created distorted desires from natural ones, that drew us and repulsed us at once. The girl stroked his hair but the desolation of that night in the city after the stoning came back to Daniel.

"We are cursed. Humans I mean." Perhaps the End hadn't been such a bad thing.

"You shouldn't hate what you are Traveller – you didn't choose it. No repentance is needed for that. The Garden is an allegory, the curse an evolutionary change. It opens up a new path just as it opens up the pit."

She paused and looked at him with pity. "Daniel, I can grant you one thing because of the way you chose. A chance to have more than knowledge. A chance to understand. But it will bring you great sadness."

"I have that already."

"That is true – but you will be free of it soon."

"I want to understand."

"I can see that." She smiled. "Alright. Then I grant you a single day. You will find it in your sleep"

Daniel felt a warm glow bind and encircle him.

"You will see what you will see and choose as you will choose. And tomorrow you will travel as I, bound to this forest, cannot." She looked for the last time into his eyes, and she was more beautiful than ever. "You will not see me when you awake but you will still be part of me until the edge of the woods, and even afterwards our fingertips will brush in the touch of grass and tree. And I will know you again when you reach your destination, Traveller." She drew close to him and kissed him, and he fell into a deep sleep.

Chapter 14

Weak light filtered through the blinds. Daniel lay motionless, with a feeling of gradually rising from a great depth. Sophie lay beside him, still asleep. An age of time seemed to separate him from her and yet, as he began to flex his fingers and toes, to feel his heart beating, to sense the warmth of the room, that time seemed to fold away, a life condensed to memories, memories condensed into a dream. He lay there for a long time, not knowing what was real. Nothing changed. The room was solid. Under the covers, Sophie's body rose and fell with her breath. After a while he got up and put on his clothes. The mantid had withdrawn among the dark leaves of its terrarium. He shut the door of the room quietly as he left and walked slowly down the steps he had so eagerly bounded up only a few hours earlier. Memories elbowed their way to the front of his mind again, events only one day old re-taking their place.

"I grant you a single day."

If it was all real. And if not?

If not, he still had Kate. He still had a job and Pemberton was still a friend. He walked down the avenue and along a path that wound through the park bordering the river. There was a hum of traffic, commuters already on the inner by-pass road. Something had happened to him. He had the memories, the experiences. And yet. A jogger ran past and on the grass a man threw a ball for his spaniel with a flexible throwing stick. And yet nothing could have happened to him. He'd spent the night with a girl and now it was morning.

He reached the river which swirled here as it narrowed before the snaking bends further south, and he sat on a bench beneath a row of weeping willows. A black-headed gull stood on a buoy near the opposite bank, preening. A cold wind ruffled its feathers. His old life began to mingle with that which had seemed to happen since. He forced himself to let them.

167

How could all those things have fitted into a single night, a single moment? The wood spirit's face was vivid in his mind. He tried to consider things calmly. What if everything could be one? If, in some way, it *was* one? Then one might have any experience in a nano-second. Like stepping through a beam that is wafer thin but another dimension wide and emerging at the other side with a new perspective. The gull leant forward and took flight, skimming the water. But then, what had directed his path through that oneness, pulled out that particular journey, that specific vision? The mantid? Some subconscious part of himself? The Green Man? He shivered. He had to admit that he had new memories, new experiences, new beliefs. They grated against the memories of his actions at the university, in his personal life. They gave him something to do. A way to be. So, what did it matter what had happened? Whether it was a dream or a vision or another reality? The only thing he could do was continue the journey. He stared into the river. So where did that take him?

It takes you to Kate.

His heart sank but he knew it was true. He would have to speak to her. He thought about it. She always got up early on Saturdays – she went for a jog before breakfast and then had a cup of coffee, sitting in that wicker chair by the window in her apartment. It was 7.30 now. She would have been up at 6.30. If he walked over there now, she would be onto the coffee by the time he arrived. Did she know he'd been with Sophie, like she had in the dream? He looked up at the trees and rubbed his face with his hands. No beard.

Half an hour later he stood at Kate's door waiting for her to answer his knock. He'd planned everything he had to say. He fidgeted with one of his coat buttons. It took her a long time to get to the hall. He could have used his key but that didn't feel right. He stared at the neat postage stamp of grass at the front of the little modern house. He could see the skeleton beneath the skin. The faux Victorian front door yielded, and Kate stood in the shadow of it, not opening it fully. He felt her anger and her sorrow all mixed up and himself at the heart of it.

"What do you want?" she asked.

"To talk to you."

"Get lost Daniel, I've had enough." She moved to close the door.

"I'm sorry". He realised he'd never said it to her before.

She stared at him for a moment, then turned back into the house. He followed her in. In the front room a big box of tissues sat on the arm of the sofa. The blanket she drew round herself to watch those movies he had always hated was on the floor and there was an empty bottle of Rosé and a half-finished glass of it on the table. She perched at the front of the armchair and he moved aside a cushion and the box of tissues and sat on the sofa.

"Well?"

"I ..." He struggled for the words he had so carefully rehearsed. "Sorry," he started, and then spoke fast. "I slept with that girl from the party last night." He stared at the tassels on the corner of the blanket. "Because I wanted to, and because I thought that my wanting it was all that mattered. But I was an idiot. That's not all that matters." He looked up at her.

"Is that it?"

"No. I have to be straight with you. I went from one extreme to the other. I can't just blame what happened to my parents for that. I was naïve and I wanted an easy answer. I wanted to have all the security of being with you and all the fun as well. Now I get it, finally. There's nothing wrong with the fun. But there is something wrong with trying to have everything. You have to choose." She started to speak but he got in first. "I know. I know. I'm telling you this like it's some amazing insight when it's just what you've tried to tell me all this time. You've been a good friend to me. But I've used you. I have to take responsibility for that." Unexpectedly his voice choked. "So, I – I have to say goodbye." The scene felt suddenly

169

distant from him.

Back outside by the little square of grass he stood and wiped his eyes. After a few moments he started to walk slowly back towards his own apartment. It was the right thing – to set her free, to let her find her place, to stop using her to fill a gap. There was only one girl who had ever really mattered to him. It had been years but, he knew she'd take him back. With her he had had that connection, more than lust, more than practicality – and now he could see it. At home he went straight to his PC – he'd waited to get home, rather than trying to locate and contact her on his smart phone and making a mistake. He opened the social media app and typed in her name – Jane Nelson. And there she was, the third hit – he recognised her instantly from her profile picture. His heart beating faster, he pulled up her home page. It was Jane alright. But in the top photo she held a baby. There was a caption above it.

'Feeling blessed with Mark Jones and our beautiful daughter.'

He sat for a long while looking at the photos that scrolled across his screen. Mark, he noticed, looked a bit like him, though more solidly built. Eventually he switched off the computer and went to lie on his bed.

Why are you trying to go backwards? Because it's comforting? Because it's certain? Have you learned nothing?

Time passed. He looked at his bedside clock – it was after twelve already. A single day. It already seemed crazy to believe that. But still, what was it that everyone always said – live every day like it's your last? Somehow the phrase seemed less banal than it used to. Pemberton would be in his office for the afternoon, he always was. Daniel got up, splashed cold water on his face at the bathroom sink. Then he hastily put together a sandwich and grabbed a bag of crisps to eat on the way. The familiarity of that task, the naturalness with which it came to him, pushed years in the wilderness further back into the world of visions. Walking through the flood, the mirror world below him and separate. He pulled on his coat and set out for the university.

It seemed to him as he walked that everything was vivid, super-granulated, detailed. The roughness of the paving stones, the colours of autumn leaves, the faces of the people he passed. He shied away from it, walking with his head down, trying to adjust bit by bit.

He stopped at the gates of the college from which a short drive across the lawn led to the gravel forecourt of the oldest part of the campus. Pemberton had had chances to move closer to his lab, to the new offices along the street but had always held on to his place here, despite the inconveniences of the old rabbit warren of offices. Daniel had gotten so used to the place over the years that he'd stopped noticing its features, but now it seemed imposing, cold. Maybe he should deal with this part tomorrow. He'd done a lot already in one day.

If there is a tomorrow. Get in there.

Pemberton's door, warped and crooked against the stonework of the wall, was ajar. That meant he was in, and that he would welcome a distraction – although, thought Daniel, maybe not from me. He knocked. As he stepped into the office at Pemberton's shout, a wave of humidity hit him; the professor was constantly misting the leaves of his towering plants and that, along with the output of a giant metal Victorian radiator, meant the atmosphere was tropical. Those plants imposed themselves so much that whenever Daniel came here, he half-expected Pemberton to be sporting a khaki safari jacket, perhaps with a macaw on his shoulder. Behind the professor, the view of the wintry lawn and the spreading Cedar through the window – reality – seemed incongruous alongside the exotics and in the damp heat of this jungle outpost. Worlds within worlds. Pemberton greeted him with a friendly hello, but he didn't look too comfortable. That party welled up in Daniel's mind. Yesterday, remember? Through different eyes he recalled the professor's reticence as he'd spouted off about love and evolution. The rest, the dinner party, Pemberton's opposition to the OPE proposal, had been part of – whatever had happened to him. Which meant this

171

was a step in the dark.

"Professor, I wondered if you had a few minutes to talk – about my OPE proposal?"

"Ah yes, the proposal. Yes, yes we need to talk about that I suppose." Daniel wondered how often before he'd made people feel this awkward. Pemberton gestured to an office chair. "Just dump those notes on the floor."

Piling the papers that had been strewn on the chair against the wall, Daniel sat at the corner of the desk. Beside Pemberton on his monitors, screensaver photos of tree frogs gently changed from one species to another.

"So, what did you want to talk about?"

"I've been thinking about my plan as it stands. And – I've had a change of heart." He shifted in his seat – he might as well just get it out. "OK, I won't beat about the bush. I've decided I want to stop this. But I don't know how to do it without ruining my reputation."

"Go on." Pemberton wasn't giving anything away, but Daniel thought he detected a softening of his penetrating gaze, a gaze that had dissected the arguments of many a post-grad student over the years. He ploughed on.

"I got carried away working out what I could get from OPE. Don't ask me why but I've started to look from a different perspective. I didn't think anything else mattered except our evolved desire. Self-interest. I thought that was what the ideas you taught me meant."

The professor stared at him for a while. "OK." He looked away from Daniel, out of the window towards the cedar. Daniel noticed a sandwich box sitting on the sill, presumably to keep the contents cool. Pemberton sighed. "OK. If that's true I should take some of the blame for it."

"No, I was naïve. I accepted it all at face value. It took a lot to make me see things differently." Nobody would ever believe what it

172

had really taken. "Anyway – the point is – the proposal would be great for me but not necessarily for the rainforest. We'd get breakthroughs, I'm certain of it, but OPE –"

"Would rip the forest apart once they were in there."

"Yes. But it's all arranged – Frank and Jill are committed, and so am I. If this doesn't go ahead – I've got no other funding options lined up. I put pretty much everything into this."

"Hmmm." Pemberton looked at him appraisingly for a moment. "I'm glad you've changed your mind on this. Your proposal had put me in a pretty difficult position. I have to say I don't understand what could have altered your point of view so fast. But people are constantly surprising."

"This doesn't cause you problems?"

"If it did, I could just run with the proposal myself, couldn't I?"

That was a jolt. Daniel had been so sure of what he needed to do that he'd taken Pemberton's 'other side' for granted – but that other side had been in his dream.

Pemberton caught his look. "Ha! That didn't occur to you did it? Well, don't look so worried. Luckily I don't quite do as I apparently say." The professor's eyes rested momentarily on a photo of his wife propped up by his keyboard.

Daniel smiled weakly. "Thank you. I'll tell Lord Denver and the others then." He started to stand.

"Hold on Daniel, hold on. I know this is serious for you. Let's think about it carefully. We might be able to do something more positive than just knocking things on the head and taking the consequences." He got up and stared out again at the sweeping branches of the Cedar. There was no sound except the gurgling of water in the central heating pipes and an echo of voices somewhere down the corridor. Daniel felt suddenly relaxed.

Over the next hour he and Pemberton talked over the issues, the options. Problems that had seemed insurmountable to Daniel

173

became manageable challenges. They looked at alternative research directions and the logistics of pursuing them. Shared with Pemberton, Daniel's ideas were worked into a new plan.

Eventually the professor threw down his pen and stretched. "OK, I think we're getting somewhere."

"You think it might work?"

"One thing at a time. I'm snowed under with this marking. While I'm busy with this you need to get stuck into the literature and work out whether this has been looked at, and if not whether it's worth us doing. All of those research ideas need to be thought about – and with the others too. But we need to get the prep right before we put it to Frank and Jill – and especially Donald – and that means acting fast before they realise the old plan is dead. Once I've worked through this lot, I'll think about some plan Bs from my back catalogue of un-resolved research questions, in case you need alternatives. And last but certainly not least we do need some money – there's a few pots I might be able to access but, you need to see what open calls are out there that we might bid for."

"I'll get onto it."

"Good. There's a lot of ways this could fall down. There's a chance though, there's definitely a chance. But Daniel, you realise – if we do ditch OPE Denver isn't going to be happy, and you do need to think about that – he knows a lot of people and OPE are behind a lot of funding calls. He's known for years to avoid me, and I was too senior for him to hold back when we first crossed swords. But at your career stage it is a risk."

"I understand that. I've got to do it though."

"OK." Pemberton gave a little nod. "Still, think about it."

Daniel stood up. "Professor – Bob – thanks for this. I – I wish we'd talked like this before."

Pemberton shrugged. "You weren't ready. You are now."

Whether by chance or through some sub-conscious direction,

Daniel's route away from the old building took him to the area of white-painted Georgian townhouses where the Peters' lived. Here was their house, unilluminated and faded compared to last night, in the throes of the party, when he'd walked away from it cursing Bill and Susanne for their meddling. Another wrong to be righted? It wasn't that simple, with them. He felt a nudge though, a little push, an echo of that call to travel that had drawn him along the pathways of his mind. He found himself at their door – just himself in the daylight – and pressed the bell. Would they be in? It was a Friday, but their parties were part of Bill's job and Daniel knew that the day after they often relaxed or worked from home. The door swung open and there was Bill, in an open necked shirt and jeans. He didn't quite start back when he saw who it was, but Daniel saw the surprise in his eyes.

"Daniel?"

"Bill. Sorry to call unannounced."

"It's a surprise to see you."

"Can I talk to you – and Susanne, if she's in."

"She's here," he stepped back to let Daniel in. "Susanne – it's Daniel." He ushered Daniel through. "Go on, into the front room – the kitchen's a mess after last night"

For the second time in twenty-four hours Daniel walked into the big front room; the furniture was still arranged for the party but in the morning light it was once more mundane, hard-edged. Bill pulled an armchair round close to one of the sofas and beckoned Daniel to sit.

"Would you like a drink of something Daniel? Coffee, tea?"

"Oh." He needed a coffee. One night without it, not years. "Yes, thanks. Black coffee, please."

Bill went out and he could hear him and Susanne talking in the kitchen but not what they said. On the wall in front of him where he sat was that painting of the hunt. It still sent a shiver down his spine, as it had the night before. Except there was something there he hadn't noticed then. Gazing at the woods towards which the fox was running, he saw another curve of pale paint. A slender figure between the trees. Was that – ?

Bill came in with Daniel's drink and set it down on the coffee table by the sofa. And now Susanne came in too, out of hostess mode, wearing joggers and slippers. Daniel remembered that she had a cycle machine.

"Daniel, I'm glad you called." She sat down next to Bill – just like those Sunday afternoon teas – but so many things had changed since then. Suddenly he saw a kindly, ageing couple who were lonely. He realised he'd never looked at them before.

"Thanks for letting me come in. I'm probably not someone you wanted to see."

"We always want to see you," said Susanne. "But ..."

"I know. I know. I've been thinking about everything. I've behaved pretty selfishly. I wanted to say that I'm sorry." He looked at them both. "I'm going to try and do things differently from now on."

Susanne smiled at him. "To hear you say that Daniel, after all this time –"

"After my parents ..." He paused.

"It's OK," said Bill. "Take your time"

"My reaction was too much. Childish. Jumping from one extreme to another."

"You were very young Daniel, remember that."

"But I pushed on with it, didn't I? I didn't listen. I ..." He looked down.

Get it all out. They deserve to know.

"At first I hated you – I thought the time I spent with you should

176

have been spent with them. And then – then my views were different. You didn't fit with them."

There was a long silence. Bill reached out and took his wife's hand. "It's good that you could say that old chap." He stopped and looked at Susanne for a moment and she nodded. "You might not have realised it, but Susanne and I have thought about this a lot too, prayed about it. We realised, after what happened to your parents, that we'd monopolised your time. We thought we were helping you out but really we ..."

"We couldn't have children Daniel," Susanne cut in. "You filled a gap." She was gripping Bill's hand tightly.

He hadn't thought of that. He didn't know what to say.

"You weren't to know what would happen."

"Thank you for saying that old chap."

Daniel paused. "I can't go back to the belief I had before though – you understand that?"

"But?" Bill always had a way of knowing when there was more.

Daniel smiled. "But I've found a belief, an understanding. Not the same as yours but not so different either, in the end."

He expected a negative reaction to that, but he didn't get one. They seemed happy. They made some small talk about the party and tidying up, the events in college the following week. Then Bill bought up the topic Daniel had been hoping to avoid.

"It's not our business I know but – how's Kate? She ..." Bill glanced at his wife. "I don't know if I should say this but what I said last night – we worry about her. Did you talk this through with her? She can be so perceptive. Was it her that made you think about all this differently?"

"No. No it wasn't. I had to find my own way through it. Or I thought I did anyway. You – you were right. I'd used her and it wasn't right to carry on like that. So, I ended things with her this morning."

"Oh Daniel," Susanne sighed. "She really cared for you. She saw something in you."

"Yes, and I took advantage of her."

"Then why not give her a chance to forgive you. If you've really changed. She deserves it. You deserve it."

Daniel hadn't considered it that way. That it wasn't just his decision. That setting her free might not be what she wanted. That it might not be what he wanted.

"Sorry Daniel," Susanne went on. "We're saying too much again. It's your life not ours. But think about it. Don't rush. Ask God."

Only yesterday that would have made him angry. Now it turned his mind back to that unity he had felt in the glade. "I wondered," he said. "If maybe next week you'd let me take you out for lunch? To catch up?"

"We'd love to do that Daniel," said Susanne.

*

The walled garden that marked the edge of the campus, across the road from the Peters' house, was all shades of brown: earth, leaves, dead plant stalks. Only in a couple of places evergreen shrubs retained their glossy foliage. A blackbird was foraging on the lawn, its beak like a lightning bolt as the bird thrust it down to grasp snaking, tiny worms. Daniel strolled, trying to be aware of it all. Kate would love the idea of the new project he'd been working on with Pemberton. He didn't encourage the thought or push it away.

By the east wall, someone was raking up leaves blown from the oak tree at the centre of the garden. Walking by it, Daniel paused and on impulse reached out to touch the bark, ribbed and stone grey. Slowly, imperceptibly, his hand began to sink into the trunk. It was not an unpleasant feeling. More like an embrace. He felt the wood around his hand like a part of himself. His whole arm sank in, the lignin and sap merging with flesh and bone. There was only the tree now – he was part of it – his head dipped into it like a swimmer dipping into water and he felt a pulse of life like a muffled drumbeat. Slowly the pulse merged with his heartbeat. There was a breeze on his face, soft grass beneath his head. Before he had even opened his eyes, tears were seeping from under his eyelids and running down his cheeks to meet the earth of the glade.

*

Daniel lay there among the flowers and the grass for a long time. The rising sun warmed the air, and the hum of bees and the swell of birdsong welcomed the new day. Perhaps if he slept again, he could get back.

No. You have further to go.

He knew it was true. Eventually he struggled to his feet and dragged his pack onto his shoulders. He left the clearing in a daze. His path it seemed, lay to the west and as he walked a wilder landscape unfolded around him. The valleys were narrower than those through which he had been walking before, their sides rising steeply to the hard, raking lines of mountains. His way took him along an old track cut deep between earth banks with twisted trees arching over it in a living tunnel. Tree sparrows squabbled in the foliage above him, but underfoot black mud made each step heavy, and he wished for the nimbleness of those fluttering birds. The little light that there was, was fractured by branch and leaf into a mosaic of colour and shade, dazzling blades of sun and black shadow.

Beneath that camouflage he only noticed the man at the last moment, huddled and motionless by the path, wearing a black hooded cowl. Wizened feet jutted out, almost skeletal, from beneath and the only sign of life was the heavy rise and fall of his chest as he laboured to breathe. Daniel fought down a sudden fear, a desire to

179

scramble up and over the earth-bank and leave this apparition to its own devices. But how could he leave someone alone in this place? As he came close the man shifted and two upturned hands were raised towards him.

"Help me." The man's words were barely a whisper.

"What do you need?" Daniel could not hide the shake in his voice. The man's face was hidden.

"I have nothing."

Daniel's pack weighed heavily on his shoulders. What it contained was more than just kit. It was his past, a part of himself; the tools were like old companions, scarred like him by use and accident along the road. They were part of his habits, part of his routine. He had killed for them. He took out some food and gave it to the man. The man grasped the food, drew it inside his shawl. And then his hands were raised again.

"Help me."

Daniel took out more food and one of his fire-lighting flints and handed them to the man. And again, they disappeared beneath the crumpled shawl and again those hands were raised.

"Help me."

He took out his mug and his mess-tin, from which he had eaten for years, a line of continuity over all that time, the feel of them in his hands so familiar, and he placed them into the scrawny hands of the stranger.

"Help me."

He took out his warm winter blanket, with the patched holes he had sewn up himself, the blanket that had been his comfort on freezing nights when the shadows of the past had pressed in on him and surrounded him, and he passed it to the man. The blanket was drawn within, but again the rasping voice came back.

"Help me."

Finally, Daniel knew what was required. With a heavy heart, he picked up his whole kit bag, weighted with his memories and his hopes; everything he owned, everything precious to him. He placed the bag into the gnarled old hands. And as the man reached forward to take it, his robe opened and Daniel saw a dark blue coat, holed and torn. The coat had brass buttons and the second of them was missing. He stepped back, in his mind the image of a magpie picking a button off the corpse of an old man –

"I'm so sorry," he whispered.

There was a silence. The man's head rose to look at him, still hidden beneath the hood. Suddenly a burden was lifted from Daniel that he had not even been aware he was carrying. And he was alone on the track in the mud and the cold and he had no possessions and he was free.

✳

That night, Daniel found an old sheep pen of sturdy, dry-stone walls to rest within. It lay at the head of a valley with a wide green sward of open ground rising behind it, banked by bracken, and a stream that grew as it tumbled down beside the enclosure to meet the woodlands below. He gathered some of the bracken as bedding, stacking it against the stones where he would be warmest.

It's going to be a cold night.

But glancing up, something caught his eye. Stuck into a crevice in the half-collapsed wall were a fire-lighting flint and steel, and below, in another crevice, a package of leaves. He reached out and took them, unwrapping the leaves and finding within two fish, some bread.

'And its fruits will be shown to you and its ways will be open to you.'

The next day Daniel followed his path with renewed strength. He found he was not afraid anymore of being seen. He stayed up on the ridges or contoured the hills, making fast progress. Conifer plantations replaced deciduous woodlands. Streams and rivers were bright ribbons far below him along glacial valleys curving south and east. Although it made for harder going, Daniel welcomed the change; to return to the mountains felt like coming home, the vastness of their embrace making their protection seem more certain.

Sometime in the afternoon he was traversing a hillside among scattered trees. As he emerged from the woods onto open grassland a flurry of rain blew in from the north. Below, he caught sight of the tall, elegant arches of an abbey, a romantic ruin on the banks of a wide river, about it the bowl of the valley, the sweep of woodlands set out like an 18th century landscape painting, nature and human endeavour on a grand scale. Closer to him on the slope a stone crucifix gazed down silently at the scene. The rain cloud passed him, moving out to cast a curtain of grey across the vale, mist rising as the sun shone once more, soaking the ground with drops of light. Water trickled down the stone face of the figure on the cross. Over the years its flow had worn his features, sent dark tracks down his body, down the pale frame on which he hung.

Suddenly, sensing something close to him, Daniel looked round. With a thrill of fear, he found that the Green Man was standing beside him, his presence exuding the life that the monument lacked.

"It is not what you think," the man said. "You think that this is false. Your faith in Him is gone."

"It is, but ..."

"But you are not sure. There is something about Him, isn't there? Stuck there, suffering, as life cycles around Him?" The Green Man gazed at the figure, with an unfathomable look in his eyes. Bands of light and shadow rippled across the valley below, illuminating the stillness of trees and fields, glinting back off the river, making the stone of the abbey glow. That stillness over which the light played was an illusion. On the trees, too distant to be seen, leaves danced in the breeze, casting off showers of sparkling rainwater. In the fields and woods insects crawled and flew and burrowed, shrews and hedgehogs foraged. Growth and decay, accretion and erosion, followed their irresistible courses.

The Green Man turned to him. "You feel it. The mind that emerged at one threshold seeks another. But you cannot make it all fit." He pointed with his staff, down at the foot of the cross. "Look more closely."

Daniel crouched on the turf. He noticed that the stone was lined, almost like tree-bark. He followed the lines upward and the greyness was tinged with brown, and above –

He started back. The legs of the figure now emerged from living wood, and they were green with life. Where the cross beam had been were two heavy branches, weaved together with its arms, and adorned with leaves. And its face was the face of the Green Man, and leaves streamed from his mouth, and at his head was white blossom.

Daniel turned to the man, amazed, but he was gone. And when he looked back at the tree he saw only the statue, as grey and lifeless as it had been before. He stood there for a long while, staring at it. Eventually, he left the ridge, heading west. As he walked the freshness of the air, the solidity of the unfolding landscape, made what had happened seem less and less clear. What was it he had seen? Had he seen anything? 'The mind that emerged at one threshold seeks another.'

The mind might want more but that doesn't mean there's any more to be had.

I've *seen* more though.

Have you? Are you sure?

He'd chosen to travel. He'd chosen to ignore that cynical voice. But Dominic had wondered if he was real. He'd wondered himself.

Because it's not real, is it? You want it to be, but it isn't.

What is left when the seed case is cast off? What was really nurtured? Anything? How could an idea survive anything, when it wasn't anything really – nothing but a pattern of electric impulses in the flesh of the brain? He stumbled. Everything swayed, flickered. Blackness at its edges.

"No!" He tried to pull himself up. "No!" He shouted again at the swinging sky. A rushing like a gale, taking his breath. It wasn't enough. "Alright. Alright." A robin's song, a sprig of fennel. He stood straight in the turmoil. Silence. A glow spread through his body. Sunlight rippled once more over hill and dale. He walked on.

*

From that ridge, from those ancient, rain-clouded mountains, his path took him back to a more pastoral landscape. These were not the soft, sheltered lowlands he had crossed before; this land stretched to the coast and the wind blew off the sea with a wilder feel. Old lanes hid from the elements, sunk between earth banks, their sides cloaked in grass, red campion, trefoil and bedstraw, their tops crowned with gorse and thorn. Where there were settlements, the cottages were low and thick-walled, their stonework whitewashed. In the open places, trees were bent low by the wind, stretching up only where they crowded the valleys of tumbling streams.

Three days after the meeting at the cross, he reached the sea, near the southern tip of a wide crescent bay. His way forward was unclear. The evening was warm, despite the unclouded skies; the new summer had softened the nights since he left the city and in the exposed spot in which he now found himself he was grateful for that. Tired, he did not make a fire, he just gathered bracken around himself, settling in beside a grassy bank on the narrow peninsular. The waves sighed on the shingle far below. He slept, and as he slept, he had a dream that had the clarity of a vision.

They stood on the headland, he and the girl from the glade, and the night was strangely still. He looked down at his feet. From them a line of light trailed out behind him. A crescent moon lit the sky and divided it from the darkness of the land.

"What is this line?" He asked. "What am I?"

She looked at him, as she had before, and he saw again the wisdom beneath her beauty. She smiled. "We are both spirits."

He felt full and empty at the same time. "Is this the end?"

She gazed into his eyes, and he into hers. "Look."

And he saw the sea bright with fluorescence; lines of blue-white light that led over indigo waves to a dark smudge of land on the horizon, coming from all directions. Like the lines on a scallop shell, they drew together, coalescing in a silver star standing low on the back of that island. Then star and lines and light faded into night, and the wind blew again, and the waves boomed on the shore and the black water was streaked bone-white by the moon and she was gone. And he awoke.

To the east, over a chain of time-worn peaks crowned with cairns, the sky was rose pink. The ground before him was grey with morning mist, the sea below as grey as the mist, heavy and solid in a rolling swell, rushing and dragging at the shingle. Without its star the island was grey too, lifeless. Out in the channel a band of deceptive smoothness marked a powerful tidal race. He clambered down from the embankment onto a road pierced by fists of dandelions now gone to seed. His step did not disturb their feathered heads. The road finished at a concrete apron, broken off jagged on a pebble beach where the greys and browns of sea-smoothed rock were edged with kelp. A fishing boat lay grounded in the shallows, over on its side, barnacle covered, holed and with traces of blue paint peeling from its woodwork.

Crossing the beach to the edge of the waves he paused. What was he doing here? Following a dream? But what else was there to follow?

At the shore, he took off his clothes and left them on the stones.

The cold of the waves took away his breath, but no matter. He began to swim. The water touched every nerve with cold, shouted to his senses through the hard breeze, the fleck of rain, the call of gulls. Yet nothing seemed real. His mind was full of thoughts of his journey. It sought freedom from structure and from words, from the barriers they form; the freedom to reach out, to be part of something that was him and the girl and everything else, and that search had a pull as great as a spring tide. But the distance to the island's shore, which from the cliffs he could have covered with his thumbnail, was from among the waves an apparently un-crossable void. The low, dark form of his destination seemed not to change, not to come closer, although he felt the water slipping by. Had he timed it wrong? Was the flow not a mark of his progress but the run of the tide? A seal bobbed to the surface close by him, its dark eyes calm though around it the sea was all movement, and it seemed to ask him: "Why are you here?"

When it dived, he suddenly sensed beneath him the unseen world that he floated above, crossing its silver-studded sky, exposed and vulnerable. And the land behind was a blur starred by diamond-hard sunlight and the land ahead was a blur starred by soft-falling raindrops. They pricked the smooth waves, an element finding its own, each drop absorbed, its journey having an inevitable end that mistaken choice could not deny. The pattern was set, the consummation certain, the journey through the air like a train ride through a land that changes and shows its character, but which you cannot explore – a line carrying the passenger to his fulfilment, despite his fear.

The constant inevitable fall of rain, the satisfaction of natural order, calmed him and his stroke was surer through the gentle fizz of water-on-water. The blur of the island ahead became more solid and his fears of drifting and floundering and drowning dissipated as he progressed, and he was SURE. Even if the currents had started to flow again, he was past their strongest force. He had chosen the moment well. The certainty of reward was a glow, making his doubt seem such an insignificant barrier that he wondered why it had held

186

such power. He had broken through, crossed the divide, and his goal was close.

With heavy limbs, he moved towards the mouth of the haven. The sun was rising, and its light seemed to reflect off something up on the headland – a standing stone. He guessed it must be covered in something – metal maybe – to shine so brightly. But no, the angle was wrong for that. It was as if the light was radiating from the stone itself. Around him puffins whirred and in their wake silver dust shimmered in a trail, trimmed to the pattern of their flight. Shearwaters, late returning, cut the wave tips with their slender wings and shards of green danced and shone, and where the gannets dived like shafts of white light, turquoise stars blossomed up and hung suspended. Fish glinted below him and shed gold scales from their weaving shoals. As his hands passed through the water, they too were trailing light. Seals swam close by him as he neared the shore, their glow a languid deep blue. From a distance when they rose to the surface their dark wide eyes watched him with a cautious welcome. They saw that the light was with him too, and that he saw it, and their whiskers glittered sapphire.

On the beach, he found the pebbles kept a reddish glow of their own, beyond that given by the early morning sky. Gulls swerved high up and scarlet like flame rippled in their wake and faded on the air. He walked up the slope, his line of light pale ahead of him. And now on the winding track beside him, on the hillside, he saw other shadows walking too, and saw the lines that trailed out from them, like in his dream. Now the shining stone was before him and all besides seemed darkened, except his own line of light that was ever brighter.

The Golden Man lay in a small, plain room. He was dying. The room was somehow familiar, and the Golden Man was somehow familiar. Inside the Golden Man's head, the chasing particles of light fought back the seed of unity, that wave of light that wanted to reach out beyond its cage of flesh and bone. Particles and whole, isolation and oneness, fear and love, physical and that which is beyond, pushed against each other. And in their struggle, though it was a struggle only of those final seconds of the Golden man's life, Daniel saw images of his own journey: the garden at Alston, Sylvia, The Hunter, The Green Man, the woman in the glade. Then he recognised the room, and it was the room in Carl's cottage, and he recognised the Golden Man, and it was he, Daniel. Finally, he saw the whole, the wave, gain ground, subsume the racing lights and consummate its connection with what lay beyond, and the glow radiated out to be part of *the rest* and the body of the Golden Man became a forgotten shell, an empty chrysalis.

He stepped forward into the whiteness, and there was no stone, only space. And suddenly his view was not from one perspective but from all perspectives at once – like he had felt in the glade but overwhelming, all-encompassing. He was consumed by hatred within the mind of a man in pain at some deep loss, uplifted as an old woman gazing at an unfurling flower bud, felt release within the meditation of a thin, bald monk in the coolness of a temple, the bitterness of a woman sitting in an empty room, the warmth in a mother's choice to bless her child's leaving, the meanness of a man pushing past someone on a crowded pavement, the smile of a fraudster, the peace of someone's forgiveness. The hatred, the cheating, the thoughtlessness, the lust – the physical sensation of each was fading, what was left being laid bare. As the pain in her body receded the girl being stoned found care for friends buried beneath it, as the joy of lust left another there was nothing beneath but darkness. Beyond those milling feelings and thoughts and images were the shadows of all religions and none. And now those experiences expanded exponentially, and he was no longer alone and observing, but a tiny part of something greater. But no, that did not sum it up. He was not a part – that suggested division – he was in everything, and everything was in him. And everything was everything that had ever been and ever would be, and she was there and his parents and every other person and thing, but not separately.

And as his perception grew his sense of time disintegrated and everything was and…

Things did not
                    Follow in
    Time   But Just
                Were
        Together
                        Infinite
        Joy
                                Unity
        Understanding
                    LOVE